My Pet

A DIRTY BOSS ROMANCE
BOOK ONE

C.M. STEELE

THE STEELE PRESS

Jack & Petra

Nervous, scared, and completely unqualified. That's the way I walked into Jack Shaw's office building. I walked out with my stomach in knots for a completely different reason. My heart is pounding like I had actually went running.

My head and heart war with quitting or working through the fiery desire he stimulates through me. At the end of the day, I leave the decision to him. The problem is I can't tell if he wants to toss me over his desk or out on my rear. I guess by the dark look in his eyes, I'll soon find out.

CHAPTER

One

PETRA

I hold my messenger bag strap tightly to my chest as I enter the security check of a corporate building in downtown Chicago. The revolving doors limiting the cold March breeze coming through the door, but they also keep the indoor air inside.

I'm immediately assaulted with the smell of food from the first-floor café that hits my nose, making my already nervous stomach rumble. Suddenly, I regret not eating breakfast this morning. I'm not a breakfast person; today must be the exception.

I'm not sure I'm able to handle this position, but I need the money. I came all the way from the southside of the city for this job, so I can't turn around now. The trip took me forty-five minutes and a lot of stress, but it's an opportunity I can't pass up, even if I'm underqualified—seriously underqualified.

"Miss? Can I help you?" the security guard at the front desk asks. I'd been so lost in my own nerves that I hadn't noticed the woman with long black hair, about five years older than me, dressed in a dark blue blazer with the building logo emblazoned on the breast pocket.

This is a twelve-story building, which is considered average in the city. Not every building downtown is the size of the Willis Tower or the John Hancock Building.

"Yes, I'm here for my first day working for Shaw Enterprises," I speak up, finding my voice; it's weak and shaky, making me feel even more unsure of myself by the second.

"Okay. May I see some identification?" she asks, arching her brow with a bit of suspicion in her eyes that doesn't do anything to ease the first-day jitters. Although I suspect it's not her job to make me comfortable; she's here to keep people safe.

"Oh, yes," I muttered, digging through my bag for my wallet. "Sorry. One more second," I grunt while I continue the search. I can't believe I'm not prepared.

Panic shoots through me, my palms are sweating,

and I'm getting flustered until I come to my senses. I stop and slap my forehead when it hits me. It's in the front zipper for a reason—so I'd be ready for this morning. Opening it up, I hand it over to the woman, and she smiles. "I put it here so I could easily grab it."

When I look at her again, she's smiling kindly at me. "Don't worry—first-day jitters. It's best that you shake them out here anyway." She checks my ID and then looks at something on her computer for what I'm assuming is my name on a list for something.

She hands my ID back to me and then points toward the corridor. "Take this elevator up to the ninth floor. You're scheduled to meet with Linda Hoffman in Human Resources."

"Thank you. Have a great day."

"You, too. Good luck!" She seems much nicer, knowing that I'm actually not some crazy person trying to get into the building uninvited.

"Thanks. I'm going to need it," I mutter that last bit, tucking my wallet back into my bag while my low heels click toward the bank of six elevators, three on each side. I tap the up button and wait, tension only doubling in my stomach, creating a nervousness that I've never felt before.

I've been apprehensive, scared, but I've always tried to see the brighter side of things and looked at it as the next challenge in my shitty life. This is different. I feel so afraid of fucking up, like there's so much more at stake than temp work. Maybe it's because my last assignment went so terribly wrong.

I look up at the cameras hidden in the corner of the corridor and no, it's not that. My heart does a leap out of my chest, as if I can sense someone actually watching me. I know someone is, and not just the woman in the front who's probably monitoring all the cameras, but someone else.

The elevator doors ping and open, shaking me out of those silly thoughts. Ignoring that train of thought, I press the button for the ninth floor and then take a calming breath before it comes to a stop.

When I step off, I'm greeted by a hallway and a set of glass doors that say Shaw Enterprises Administration Offices. I walk through the doors and see a receptionist who tosses a friendly smile my way. "You must be Miss Novak."

"Yes, I am." I smile, giving no sense of my underlying nervousness. It helps that she's not the boss and I'm not under her specific scrutiny.

"Linda will be out in a minute to retrieve you. Would you like a bottle of water, juice, or coffee?"

"I'll have orange juice, please."

"Yes, just one minute. I'm Casey, by the way."

She shakes my hand, and I already feel a little more at ease. Looking around the small lobby on this floor, it gives me a very neutral feel. It could use some color, but I guess since this is an administrative floor, it's not a big deal, but the beige walls are pretty drab.

She comes back a minute later with a bottle of Minute Maid Orange Juice and smiles as she hands it to me before looking behind me. "Ah, here she is."

"Petra? I'm Linda Hoffman, the human resources director. Please follow me." She's equally as friendly as Casey and I don't feel as shitty as I did when I first came in, although I'm a bit overwhelmed the second she mentions who I'm working for.

"Mr. Shaw? As in Shaw Enterprises?"

"Yes, didn't the agency inform you that you'd be working for the CEO and owner?" She directs me to take a seat while she takes hers.

After she sits, I answer her question. "No, only that I would be a temporary assistant with the opportunity to become a full-time hire if I fit in with the company."

She smiles with an apology in her eyes. "Ah, well, yes. I suppose they didn't want to overwhelm you with that idea of working for the big boss."

Linda goes through her drawers and pulls out small stack of papers and then continues. "It's going to be fine. I'm sure you'll do a great job according to your temp tests. All we ask is that if you have a problem with the boss, you inform us. He's very demanding, and it can be a lot for assistants who aren't used to the high demands."

"Oh. Okay." Now the tension is back and growing by the second. I'm grateful that my cap is sealed on the plastic container because I can feel the pressure of my hold on it.

"Relax. I'll let him know you're here." She grabs the receiver on her phone and calls him while I do calming breaths and look around the room to take it easy. It's a decent-sized office and nothing compared to what the boss will have, and yet I'm so intimidated. I can't even fathom how I'll feel when I see his massive office.

"Mr. Shaw, your new assistant will be up in ten minutes. Would you like me to escort her, or do you want Elliot to do it?" Linda says as I sit in front of her neatly organized desk.

"Just send her up," I hear him snarl on the other end of the phone.

My body has conflicting reactions to the sound. Physically, I flinch back in my chair, dropping my closed juice on the floor. Mentally, a part of me wants to run to the elevators and never enter this building again, and another wants to see if his looks match that sexy voice.

His growl is almost insanely deep, like an animal, and yet, you'd never expect that coming from the CEO and owner of a major corporation.

"Yes, Mr. Shaw." The line goes silent and she hangs up the receiver, so it's clear he hung up on her. Her cheeks flood with embarrassment, and I feel bad for her.

Damn, someone's having a pleasant day, and I'm supposed to deal with him? I'm on my second temping job, and I'm actually surprised I landed this one because I didn't think I was a good fit—although I'm not so sure I'm the one who's going to be a problem.

I'd venture to guess that Mr. Shaw goes through plenty of assistants and that's why they're willing to hire a woman from the bottom of the barrel who had quit her last job in two days because the boss got a little too touchy-feely, but most don't know that story. All anyone knows is that I quit because I was too embarrassed to deal with the judgmental eyes and comments accusing me of trying to sleep with the boss.

"I assure you he's much nicer than that on most days. He's had a rough go this morning. He's recovering from an injury caused by his last assistant, so he's not quite in the mood for a new one and, well, we're just going to make the best of it."

"What kind of injury?" I question, wanting to know if there's something I need to be made aware of, regarding his needs.

"He had hot coffee spilled down his chest and lap, resulting in serious burns," she mentions, her face scrunching up with embarrassment. I immediately imagine his bits being burnt, which is not cool at all.

"Oh. Yes, and well, let's just say she said it wasn't an accident." She squints, and I have too many questions that make me a little nervous. I want to turn on my heels and make a run for it even more now.

"Relax. He's not some pervert. She was pissed because he fired her and he did it in the middle of the breakroom after he overheard her conversation with another employee. Both of them were fired, but Mr. Shaw hasn't been in a good mood since then."

Maybe because you're telling everyone that he got his private parts burned off. That might make him feel a bit salty. Although she didn't quite say his male business was injured, that's my guess and I'm assuming so does everyone else who hears that story.

"Take these papers and finish filling it out when you have time. Bring them down to me by tomorrow.

Here's your badge. It will give you access to locked doors around the building since you will be Mr. Shaw's assistant." She's on her feet, leading me out the door to the entrance of their lobby.

"Where am I going again?" I can't remember if she told me or not, so I add the again just in case.

"To the twelfth floor. Use this elevator. If you have any questions, I'm a few floors away."

She presses the button and then essentially pushes me in, and I feel like I'm being fed to the beast or something. There's a young guy on the elevator already and he gives me a smirk. Linda greets him in a rush. "Oh, hello, Elliot. This is Petra, Mr. Shaw's new assistant."

"Hello, Petra." He sticks his hand out and I shake it. He's a handsome guy, probably a few years older than me, and I have a feeling he knows he's good looking with the smug expression on his face.

"Hello, Elliot, is it?" It causes his grin to drop for a split second, but only for a moment. I have to hold back my own smirk because he carries himself with an air of cockiness that I'm sure I will see more of.

"Yes. Welcome aboard. I'll take you up there." He presses the button and the door closes as Linda waves us off. "The boss was in the middle of a call when I was up there," Elliot adds.

"Oh, that explains his quick temper." I probably shouldn't have said that, and I need to remember to think before I speak. It's been known to get me in trouble from time to time.

"Yeah, that's it," he mutters, darting his eyes downward before bringing them back to me. So that's not why he's a dick. That's just who he is, then. I'd be pissed if someone tried to destroy my body. Burns are no joke; they can kill or permanently disfigure a person.

"Well, it doesn't matter. I'm here to do a job and go home," I informed Elliot just as the door opened.

"Sounds smart." We're greeted by a six-foot-four man in a dark gray suit. Our eyes meet for just a brief moment before he whips his head toward Elliot. He's a freaking hunk: face chiseled, lightly covered in neatly trimmed, dark scruff, caramel-colored eyes, and almost black hair that's cut short with the top slightly longer and swept to the side.

"Mr. Timmons, what are you doing up here again?" I'm so glad his attention is on Elliot because I'm trying to catch my breath. Jack Shaw is sexier than his voice. I have to bite my lip to hold back the involuntary moan trying to escape from me.

"Mr. Shaw, I came to escort Petra up here," he answers the grouchy boss.

"Following orders is so damn hard around here. Get lost, Mr. Timmons, and don't come up here unless I request your services. Miss Novak, please follow me." As mad as he is, I suppose the jerk has a point. He's hot, but not a pleasant man.

"Yes, sir."

"See ya around, Petra. Maybe we'll do lunch sometime." I take Elliot's offer as another attempt to hit on me, but nothing serious of course because the guy probably flirts with anything that walks and I'm fresh meat around here.

"Out of the question," Mr. Shaw snarls under his breath. I wonder what the hell is going on, but I'm getting the impression that I won't be around here long.

"This is your desk. I'm assuming that you have a basic background in typing and all of the office software, correct?" he asks. Although I'm not sure it comes out as a question, but more of a statement of fact because that is what is required.

"Yes, sir. I have…" I cut myself off because he unbuttons his suit jacket and slides his hand into the pocket of his slacks, dragging my attention there. Fuck. I look up and continue. "I have an associate degree from the community college in business administration, so I can manage just fine with daily office tasks. Although, I'm not sure if I'm qualified to handle more than just menial tasks."

"Do you always speak your mind?" he asks, eyebrows narrowing.

"Um…I try to be honest."

He shakes his head slightly, rubbing the bridge of his nose. "Well, don't go around pointing out that you're not qualified to assist. Let me find out for myself."

I nod, feeling slightly more embarrassed to have made an ass out of myself.

"Now, take a seat and get to work on the list of tasks on your desk. Everything you need is on the notepad. I'll be in my office on a call for the next two hours, which means I expect not to be interrupted about anything at all, unless this place is actually on fire. Understood?"

"Yes, Mr. Shaw." He walks into his office, and I'm confused. Not about the job because I have no idea what waits for me at the desk, but it's more about what to make of him.

He's definitely grumpy as hell, but then he was nice enough not to fire me on the spot for being unqualified, and yet he also muttered about me not having lunch with Elliot. Maybe I'm forced to work and eat at my desk or take late lunches. Whatever.

I walk around to my desk and set my bag down before undoing the three buttons of my peacoat. I love this one—I got it two years ago at a yard sale because it's one of the few places I can find nice things for cheap. Unlike the suit that Mr. Shaw is wearing, my clothes don't cost a fortune.

I worked my butt off while attending college. Thankfully, it's the one blessing of growing up poor. I went to school for nothing and I could have gone to a four-star institution, but I would have had to take out loans and I didn't want to eat debt when I already knew what it was like to struggle to pay basic bills.

Mercifully, this job landed in my lap, and I'm going to do my best to keep it even if my boss isn't a cinnamon roll. In fact, he's the opposite of it, which I assume is something burnt and bitter, but I need to stop thinking about that chisel-jawed jerk and focus on what he left for me.

It's a list of passwords to log in and a small to-do list. All of it seems straightforward, so I get to work. I'm midway through it when the phone rings. Unfortunately, no one told me how to answer it, but I do my best. "Mr. Shaw's office, how may I help you?"

"Petra, this is Linda. I'm just seeing if everything

is okay." I'm surprised she's calling and the nervous pitch in her voice.

"So far, so good. I've gotten through some of his list here, but I'm not sure what else he'll have left to do and he's asked not to be disturbed because he's on a call."

"Good. I'm glad. Elliot said he was a little worried about you." What a little tattletale. That's another trait to add to his list, but it's nice that he was concerned.

"I can handle myself against the big old grumpy man. Tell Elliot I'm perfectly fine." A grumble comes from beside me, and I don't need to look to know it's Mr. Shaw standing there. "I've got to go, Linda." I hang up the phone and turn to him. "I'm sorry, Mr. Shaw. Do you need me for something?"

"Did you not hear your notifications going off?"

"Notifications?"

"Yes. These?" He reaches around me with his entire body engulfing my frame to wiggle my mouse, and there's a chat box at the bottom of my computer screen that's blinking with a ten in parentheses.

"Shit. I'm in trouble."

"That you are. I'll get the files myself. Now, next time, pay attention to the notifications and turn the volume up on it if you have to. Understood?"

"Yes, sir."

"Good." He grabs something from the drawer beside my desk inches from my legs and then walks back into his office, grumbling something to himself as he closes the door.

"Way to go. Pissing off the boss on the first day," I mutter, trying to stop the shaking throughout my entire body. Why is he such a handsome ass? Why did I have to make a fool of myself?

I see a ding on the computer and check it, but it's not from Mr. Shaw. It's from Elliot. *Hey, sorry about the boss man. I hope I didn't get you in trouble. If you'd like, I can make it up to you with dinner tonight.*

I should say no, but I'm mad at the jerk boss, so I look around to see if he's looking before I turn back to my computer and respond.

Yes, I'd like to go to dinner tonight.

A minute later, his office door opens. "Miss Novak, please come into my office—now."

Two

JACK

I stare at the message wondering who the fuck this is for, getting angrier by the second because I know damn well it's not for me. A snarl comes from my throat, forcing my client to ask, "Do you need a drink, Mr. Shaw?"

"Sorry, the air must be a little dry in here." I clear my throat intentionally. "Let's continue this later on in the week after I have a chance to review the figures."

"Sounds good to me. Have your assistant contact me with the time."

Feeling irrationally possessive of her time and attention, I blurt out, "I'll contact you directly. She's new and doesn't have a clue what's going on here." It would have come off as condescending and rude if she had heard, but I don't care. The less men breathing in her scent the better for everyone involved.

"Okay. That's fine by me." We end the call and I set down the receiver, staring at my screen and the message that she accidentally sent to me, but it's already too damn late.

I stand up and walk over to the door and stop, feeling a ridiculous urge to demand that she have dinner with me to make up for this message, but that's wrong in so many fucking ways. I shouldn't want her time. I don't want her, or so I tell myself. Instead, I take my ass back to my chair and sit down.

She's beautiful. I noticed it the second she stepped into the building over an hour ago. I grew impatient as I waited for her to get up here from HR.

Since the incident with my previous assistant, I've had cameras installed in additional areas along with access for myself including the main entrance, the breakroom, and her desk. I have multiple ways now to keep an eye on my stunning assistant and for all the wrong fucking reasons.

Seeing her smiling sweetly at Elliot only made my

mood sour even more as the elevator doors opened. I hadn't wanted another assistant to work for me, but I needed one. It's hard to find a quality one, and here comes one with nowhere near enough experience. Worse, she makes me want to bend her over my desk and take her home to meet my parents, if I had parents.

I look over to her desk and she's smiling as she works, unaware that she sent the message to the wrong person. I already have a feeling who invited her: the only other asshole she encountered since she stepped into my building.

I open my office door because I don't trust myself to walk out there. "Miss Novak, please come into my office, now."

She flinches and then bites on that bottom lip. Fuck, I don't know what to do with her. I can't fire her just yet because I do need an assistant, plus I'd lose the opportunity of seeing her beautiful face every day, but I can't have her fucking dating the asshole downstairs.

"Coming," she calls out, and unfortunately my mind goes straight to the gutter. Thoughts of her pussy creaming around my fingers, tongue, and mouth play in my head, so I sit my ass back in my chair before she sees my raging hard-on, which is stretching out the seam on my pant leg.

I just tuck my legs under my desk when she steps up to the door. "Come inside and close the door, Miss Novak."

"Yes, Mr. Shaw." She clamps her lips shut and then turns to do as I request, giving me a small peek at her tight ass wrapped in a pencil skirt that hugs her perfect baby-making hips.

"Have a seat." Once she's settled, I take a deep breath. "Do you know why I asked you in here?"

"Because I've messed up again." She twists her lips before biting down on the bottom edge again.

"That's correct. Now, I'm sure that you understand this is a professional place of business, correct?"

"Yes, sir."

"Then you know making dates on company time isn't acceptable." It will never be acceptable unless all those dates are with me, but I can't say that or she'll be down in human resources filing a complaint.

"I just…shit. I'm fired." She drops her head, shoulders slumping, and I feel like a dick.

If it had been anyone else, I wouldn't care and merely sent a warning that they were contacting the wrong person because it was clear she was only responding to a message she received. Elliot's the one starting shit.

"As much as I should fire you, no. I need someone to do a job. Although if you do go out with Elliot, I will fire you. I need you to act like a professional, which means staying away from my employees. Can you do that?"

"Yes, of course. I'll just tell him no," she answers meekly.

"No. Don't bother. I will do it for you." I don't want her talking to him at all.

"Please don't fire him. He was just trying to be nice to me."

"I'm sure that's his only motivation. Now, enough wasting time talking about Elliot. I want you to get back to your desk and handle your assignments. I have too much on my plate to be reminding you to stay on task, Miss Novak. I'd hate to send you packing so soon, but I can't have you setting me further behind than I already am."

"Yes, Mr. Shaw." She nods her head, looking so meek and submissive. I've never been so damn turned on in my life.

"Good, now go ahead and finish your to-do list. I'll be having a business lunch."

"What time is my lunch hour, sir?"

"You will be accompanying me to take notes," I add, hating the idea of her having lunch with anyone else. My last assistant had an affair with one of the other employees and although I didn't give a fuck about them together, I knew they met while having lunch in the breakroom.

"Oh. That explains why I can't have lunch with Elliot." She's still thinking about missing out with that little prick. Does she like him?

"Lunch, dinner, fucking breakfast. Any fucking meal with him, and I'll make it his last one. Now, please, go finish up. I'm getting a headache."

"Sorry." She stands and then gives me a sheepish smile. I want to kick my own ass for slipping up like that and losing my temper. This time I only watch her upper body, shoulders slumped as she leaves my office, appearing broken by my harshness.

Still, I argue with myself that I have the right to be pissed. She's fraternizing on company time like I'm not right here. I'm trying to work, and she's giving her attention to the mail boy like he's worth losing her job over and I'm chopped liver. Fuck, I hate that expression, and now I'm using it.

I call in my friend Landon and ask for a favor, and then I return to my work as best as I can until it's lunchtime.

When I step out into the hall, there's a stack of mail on the desk that she's sorting through. It's the past two days' worth that I haven't bothered to look at because most of it isn't of interest. "Anything important in there?"

"That's the problem. I don't know anything about the company to know what's important yet. I've sorted the junk mail from the letters and large envelopes."

"Okay. Well, they can wait until we return from lunch. Get your coat. It's cold out." She slips on a decent peacoat. It's pretty, but it's not going to do much to keep her warm. "Where are your hat and gloves?"

"I accidentally left them on the train on my way in."

"What am I going to do with you?" I grumble to myself.

"It was a little warm on the train, so I took them off and I didn't remember until I was already on the platform and the train rolled away."

"A scarf?" I question, needing her to be warm.

"I forgot that one at home this morning." She gives me a bit of a shrug.

"Are you always this forgetful?"

"I was a bit nervous today."

The way I've been snipping at her every second, I can't blame her for that. "I suppose you have a case for it. Come on. Let's get going before the weather picks up."

We enter the elevator and thankfully are completely alone. My driver is waiting for us down in front of the building, so I shoot him a message without Petra being able to see. *Ms. Novak isn't for viewing pleasure. Understood?*

He quickly responds. *Yes, Sir.*

By the time we make it out of the lobby and onto Lake Shore Drive, the harsh wind hits us. I can see her shivering already, and I don't like it one bit, so I throw my scarf around her neck.

I take a look at her outfit and immediately send a message to my sister, asking for a favor. Marilyn sends me a stream of messages with other questions that I tell her aren't appropriate because it's just business, but my sister can be difficult.

It's a warning, a subtle, but unmistakable warning that Petra is not to be stared at in any damn way. It's nuts how possessive I am of a woman who is just supposed to be my assistant. There is no helping it though.

God, instantly I know that bringing her is a mistake unless I plan on making her mine. Heaven help me, but there are so many ethical codes, violations, and such that I'll be committing if I pull her into my arms and throw her legs over mine to straddle me as I claim her mouth. And yet…it's all I want to do.

CHAPTER
Three

PETRA

I swear the car feels like it's a thousand degrees. It doesn't help that he gave me his scarf, which is the epitome of a gentleman, and I wanted to moan because it smells of him, like sandalwood and fresh linen.

I want to climb onto his lap and ride him all the way to wherever we're planning to go. It's stupid because at my last job, I quit fast as hell for my boss trying something like that, but here I want my boss to do the same thing. Jack Shaw could maul me, and I would welcome it.

A low growl rumbles from his chest and I turn to see him typing away on his phone, so I know it has nothing to do with me. He probably has a supermodel girlfriend who sent him a sexy text. I know I would send him naughty texts at work if he was around other bitches all day. I'd be so damn jealous and seeing red.

I take off his scarf in the car because it's getting hot and hold it out for him. "Here, Mr. Shaw. Thank you, but it's quite warm in here."

"I'll hold onto it until we leave. I don't want you to lose it, after all." He smirks at me, and I'm caught off guard by the killer smile that amplifies his already insane animal magnetism.

"Was that a joke, Mr. Shaw?" I ask.

"I'm not an asshole all the time."

"I'm not touching that one with a ten-foot pole. I'm trying to keep my job."

"Wise, Miss Novak. Wise."

"We're here," he says when the car pulls off to the side and comes to a stop. The driver opens the door a moment later and helps me out of the vehicle while Jack slides out right behind me.

"Come—my client is meeting us here. All I need you to do is be quiet, take notes, and enjoy your lunch. You're not familiar with the company, so it's best to avoid all talk for now."

"Why am I here again?" I ask with a bit too much sass in my tone.

I swear he wants to spank me. "To be a smart ass, apparently."

"Ah, a job requirement I can fulfill." He actually chuckles, which makes his ass even sexier.

I'm in trouble.

I turn to the door and then gasp because the man we're meeting happens to be my ex-boss. How in the world is this possible? Now I'm really in trouble.

"Mr. Shaw, it's good of you to meet me here." They shake hands, but Dickerson hasn't taken his eyes off me. "Petra, I didn't expect you to go running to the competition," he says with a wink.

"Um…this is where the temp agency sent me."

"You know him," Mr. Shaw growls. Mr. Dickerson gives me a knowing look as if he's reading more into Mr. Shaw's reaction.

"I only worked for Mr. Dickerson's office for a couple of days, but it didn't work out."

"Well, let's sit down and get this meeting over with," Mr. Shaw says, leading the way to the table. His hand lightly presses to the small of my back just long enough to create a separation between Dickerson and myself. A change seems to come over Mr. Shaw, and I wonder if he thinks I'm a spy or something.

They talk about nothing important while we order our food. I might not know much about their businesses, but I can tell that Mr. Shaw refuses to talk shop in front of me. In fact, it's almost as if he's intentionally avoiding it.

Feeling an overwhelming sense of discomfort with Dickerson leering at me like he did while I worked for him and Mr. Shaw's stern jaw.

"Excuse me. I need to use the ladies' room." Mr. Shaw slides out of the way so I can exit the booth and then I walk away, wanting to throw up what little I could manage to eat of my lunch.

I stay in the bathroom a lot longer than I should, but I'm doing my best to hold back the tears. I'm going to get fired for nothing today. There's a commotion outside of the bathroom, and that's when I hear my name being called by Mr. Shaw. "Petra."

"One minute," I call out, trying to wipe my face.

"Now, or I'm coming in there." He wouldn't dare.

"Sir, you can't go in there. That's the women's bathroom," I hear a man say to Mr. Shaw.

"The hell I can't." Is it terrible that I'm tempted to test him? Probably. Still I think better of it and remember that I'm in the middle of a public place and don't want to cause a scene.

"I'm coming, I'm coming." I open the door before he has the chance to storm inside, and I can see that his expression has changed. He's gone from grumpy to full of concern.

His hand reaches out to mine, taking it and giving it a forceful yet harmless tug that sends my feet off balance. I jerk slightly and then fix myself. "Come on, we're leaving."

A man stops in front of us, blocking our exit from the hall off the main dining area. "Miss, you don't have to leave with him if you don't feel safe."

"She's more than safe with me." Mr. Shaw stares at the man for a moment, moving around him.

"You just punched a man in the face." I let out a gasp, coming to a complete stop.

"Well, he had it coming," he states as a matter of fact with a shoulder shrug.

"You hit him?" I ask, turning to my boss like he's lost his mind. Jack Shaw looks like he's hiding brawn under that suit, but it surprises me that he'd use it especially when it comes to a business meeting.

"He said and did something I didn't like. Are you okay?"

"I'm fine. Are we going back to the office, or should I just walk to the train station?" I ask him. I have my things so it's not like I can't just do myself a favor and avoid the walk of shame before I'm canned.

"What do you mean?" He pauses and stares at me

right inside the front doors of the restaurant as I put on my coat.

"I'm sure I'm fired."

He tilts his handsome head, squinting his eyes. "Fired for what?"

"Well, it's clear you think I'm some sort of spy since you were obviously avoiding talking business with him."

He shakes his head. "I was doing my best to be civil and not beat his ass on the spot, but I decided right then and there I wasn't doing business with him, and it had nothing to do with you being a spy. Petra, you couldn't be a spy if you tried. You have a bad habit of saying shit out loud."

"You've got a point. Or it could be a tactic," I offer, not helping my situation.

"That could have had you out on your ass the second you walked into the office this morning." He pushes the door, leading me out onto the sidewalk.

"Good point." There's an overcast right now and I'm getting the best look at him that I've had since we arrived and my heart continues to dance in my chest. Maybe it's because he's hot and being nice now.

"Get in." He holds the door open, silently telling his driver to get back inside the car.

"I'm not a spy. Just in case you had doubts. So why did you punch him?"

"Never mind why I clocked that piece of work, but I can see why you quit. He was leering at you the second we reached the door."

"Was he that obvious?" I ask. It was clear to me, but I hoped that it wasn't so blatant.

"Yes."

"I didn't sleep with him no matter what he said." I have to correct it for my own sake more than for my job..

"I didn't think you did, but it's not my business."

"I know, but I still wanted to say that because of the whole thing with Elliot. I'm not, like, going around trying to hook up with every office guy I meet. I swear."

"That's fucking good to know." He tugs at his tie, loosening it a bit, tension flowing through him.

Four

JACK

Rage beats on my brain, demanding I get my pound of flesh for Petra sake. I try to be calm when she admits they didn't fuck, but I'm relieved because I would have more than punch the fucker if she caved to his seduction game. I would have killed him without a doubt.

There would be nothing left of that fucking playboy Dickerson. He's used to bagging chicks who are too afraid to tell him no, but my girl—I mean my assistant—did just that.

Fuck, I can't be like that asshole now more than ever. No wonder I make her uncomfortable and nervous. She dealt with that bastard and then came to work for me. My rude, domineering ass has been trying to stop her from seeing a nice kid like Elliot.

He would honestly be good for her. Of course, that's if I let him live for putting his hands on her. God, I'd have to kill him if he kissed her. I'm losing my mind.

We drive back to the office in silence because I'm still heated from the fight with Dickerson. He had it coming. Luckily, he threw the first punch when I took a cheap shot at his little dick size. A man like him who has a nasty habit of forcing or coercing women must have a little pecker, so I called him out on it and he took the bait.

He shouldn't have called my woman, my assistant, an easy lay. I mentally correct myself because I can't seem to remember that she's not mine and that we don't even know each other. Still, I feel a closeness to her that I can't explain. A yearning so strong that is almost unbearable.

I should pull her records and learn more about my woman, but maybe I'll coax it out of her as we work together.

As we enter the lobby of the building, she says, "So I've finished everything on the list for today. Is there more you want me to do?"

"Yes, there's a stack of filing that has been building up, but I have no time to work on it."

"Okay. I can handle that when we get back." I press the button and the elevator doors open. Waving my hand, I tell her to go inside first. Our ride is too short and we'll soon have to separate. We reach our floor and I hold the door open for her.

"Did you eat enough? You hardly touched your food." I can't stop myself from following her to her desk like a puppy. If I had a tail, it would be wagging right now.

"I'm fine. I don't usually eat a lot." I'm betting it's because she doesn't have a lot to eat. She's working a temp job and is very young, which means she's probably on the broke side of things right now. I could fix that for her in a heartbeat, but it's not my place, so I'll do what I can until it's my place.

"Get settled, then come into the office and I'll show you how it's organized."

"Okay." She smiles softly at me. "What are these?" That's when she notices the stuff I had picked out while we were at lunch.

"Oh, they dropped them off. Good. I thought you could use a new set." She picks up the matching hat, scarf, and glove set from Macy's. It goes perfectly with her navy coat.

"Thank you, but you shouldn't have."

"I don't want you to get sick, so it will do a world of good for the both of us."

She throws her arms around me and quickly remembers herself before I even get a chance to react.

Fuck, I missed my opportunity to pull her in for a hug. Maybe it's for the best because the elevator doors open up and Landon Black appears.

I walk over to greet him. "Ah, thanks for coming by. I'm glad you could take the time out of your busy day. How's it going?"

"Great, my friend. I'm about to hunt down my woman, but I came to handle that matter you requested." I'm curious, but I don't ask because Landon's a very private man.

I make introductions a little less reluctantly, knowing he's chasing after a woman. "Landon Black, this is my assistant, Petra Novak."

"Hello, Miss Novak."

"Hello, Mr. Black. Would you like something to drink?" I introduce them only because it's polite, but I want to growl when she smiles at him.

"No, thank you." My eyes scan his face for any interest in her, but he doesn't pay any special attention to her.

"We'll be in my office."

"What about that project?" Petra blurts out before biting her bottom lip.

"It can wait. Just give me an hour." She nods and then walks back to her desk.

"Yes, Mr. Shaw." I turn back to Landon and then escort him into my office, closing the door behind me.

As soon as we take our seats, a giant grin spreads across his face. "So, I see why you were in a rush for me to get over here."

"So let me get this straight. You want a guard, a female one?"

"Yes. Of course. You trusted Danny, but there's no way I'm trusting any man around her. I don't want her to fall in love with anyone else before I can win her. Besides, she's been harassed by Dickerson."

"That asshole. I hate him. I could deal with him once and for all." We all know him because he runs in our circles, burning bridges with those who don't need his business or respect his behavior.

"No, people would suspect me right off the bat. I clocked the bastard today at the Plaza."

"Wow, I'm shocked, but then again, if it has to do with your future wife, then I'm not. I'm assuming she will be your future wife, right?"

"Of course."

"Well, then, I hope for the best. Also, the tracking device is here. Slip it into anything of hers when you get a chance. If you want me to put it in her phone, that's easy too. I'll also drop off a company phone in the morning." He winks. The fucker is super slick and that's why I need his assistance.

"Great. I want to be able to keep tabs just in case."

He raises a brow, smirking. "Just in case she finds someone else."

"That's not it." It's one of the main reasons without a doubt, but it's not my sole purpose in having someone protecting her.

His smirk turns into a full grin. "Okay. Keep telling yourself that. We all do." He stands, stretching out his hand for me to shake. I walk him out and then call her into my office, knowing he'll set up her cell while we're in the office.

"Sorry about that."

"Oh, it's okay. You're the boss, and you're a busy man. I'm at your disposal. Besides, I get paid either way, work or no work."

"Can't beat that."

"Nope." If she was my wife, she could. She could have whatever she wanted at the tips of her fingers, and all she'd have to do is ask.

By the end of the day, I know one thing: I'm crazy about Petra and I have to find a way to make her see that she belongs with me. But, until she gives me a way in, I can't just jump the gun. She's been through one sleazy boss and doesn't need another.

PETRA

"Val, I need a drink," I huff, collapsing down on our dilapidated sofa we got on for pennies on the dollar at a yard sale. Again, it's our favorite way to shop when you're poor. Valentine and I are best friends and have been for a long time.

"I got you, girl." She hits the cabinet and brings out a bottle of Smirnoff, waving it in her hand. We save that for only special occasions, and today is one of them because it's been one hell of a day.

"Tell me what happened. How did it go?" She grabs two plastic cups and the orange juice from the fridge. Although with the way I'm feeling, it might be a shots kind of night—no chasers needed.

With a dramatic sigh, I throw my arms out and hit the sofa cushions. "It was a freaking insane roller coaster. I made a mess of things from the start."

"Here. Take this, and then let it all out." She hands me the mixed drink that I quickly take a long gulp from while she plops down beside me with her own drink in hand. I begin to tell her all about my day, and then I get to my description of Mr. Shaw and his behavior throughout the day and she stops me.

Taking the cup from my hand she sets it on the table and turns her body toward me even more. Grabbing my hands in hers, she stares me right in the eyes. "Girl, are you blind?"

"What do you mean?"

"I mean—your boss has the hots for you." I think she's lost it for sure because there's no way in hell that Mr. Jack Shaw has anything going on for me.

"What? No, he doesn't. In fact, he seemed more and more irritated with me."

"Actually, he seemed more and more irritated that other men wanted your attention, but that's about it. Trust me when I say that his interest in you isn't purely work related. He beat up Dickerson, and you know it had something to do with you even if he didn't elaborate on it."

She has a point there, but civility and decency

could be behind it. "You're right, but maybe he was just being a gentleman."

"Please—he didn't risk getting arrested and sued because he was being a gentleman. He's in the public eye and wealthy. Not to mention he bought you a new set of winter wear while you went out to lunch as if it was terribly cold." It wasn't that bad in fact, I'd been warm enough to take them off in the first place. Also he did give me his scarf right away when that first chilly breeze hit me.

"What am I supposed to do?" I question, my stomach turning with nervous anticipation.

"Do you want him?"

Biting my lip, I know the answer, still I hesitate. "I do, but it's complicated."

"What's complicated? Are you afraid that it's just lust? Or a one-night stand?"

"Exactly." She reads me like a book, and that's why we've been friends forever or maybe it's because we've been besties for as long as I can remember.

We met in school. Her parents weren't the warmest people around and I grew up in a foster home until I was sixteen. It's been a rocky life, but we always have each other's backs.

"So then you play your games. Slowly test the waters, push his buttons and see what he does. If he's willing to risk it, then maybe he wants more than a fling. He's not the kind of man who can afford to risk a lawsuit for sexual harassment."

I polish off my large glass of vodka and orange juice and confidently answer, "Fine. Tomorrow I'll test him."

M y head is throbbing, but I take a couple of pills with water and get ready for work. It's going to be a long day especially because I don't know how to tempt a man, so I'm just going to play it cool. My "beer balls" have gone and yesterday's plan of temptation has fled my brain.

"That's not sexy enough," Val says as I walk out of my bedroom.

"I'm not sure I can pull off this whole game."

"Then just go in looking like the hot assistant. Trust me, that's all that's needed. The man's tongue will have to be picked up off the floor by the end of the day."

"I think you read too much." We both read too much when we're not working.

"I've got nothing better to do. Now come with

me." We go into the bathroom and she pulls out her curling wand.

"I don't have time for this." I try to walk out, but she drags me back into the bathroom.

"I'm not doing all your hair. Chill out. Five minutes, I promise."

Five minutes later and my red hair has pretty curls layered throughout and just enough to give my hair some life. She also added some deep red lipstick. "It's the all-day kind. You're welcome." She winks and pats my ass. "Go get him."

"You are ridiculous. Remind me to return the favor one day."

"If you land him, damn right I want you to return the favor."

The entire trip to the office I'm nervous and I fiddle with my phone in my hand. It's not a great one, but it's all I have.

A text comes in from Val. ***Have a good day, sweetheart***. Followed by a heart emoji.

I do my best not to laugh because she knows I'm nervous. Suddenly my nerves have disappeared and I'm feeling a bit bubbly. I can do this because all I have to do is act normal.

I reach the office building and step inside, smiling at the security guard. "Good morning Miss Novak."

"Good morning," I say.

"Has Mr. Shaw arrived?" I ask, hoping that I'll have a moment to breathe before he shows, but I get a quick nod.

"Yes. He's here already."

"Thank you." Damn, I don't know how to react to his presence. It was easier yesterday when I didn't know what to expect and even then I was frightened.

Taking the elevator up to his floor, I rock back and forth on my heels nervously, fidgeting with the gloves he bought for me. It's not like I needed them today because the temps are starting to change outside, but I love them anyway.

I open my jacket because it's getting hot. My outfit is a little on the risqué side today. Nothing unprofessional, but my buttons on the top of my blouse are open and the ones at my chest are being tested.

As soon as the elevator dings open, I collide into my boss who catches me in his big strong arms. I look up and read a heavy scowl on his face before he sets me on my feet. "Oh goodness. I'm sorry."

"It's okay. I was going to get some breakfast. Do you want anything?" I'm starving but I couldn't eat a bite with the way my stomach is rumbling.

"No, thank you."

"Fine. I'll be back in just a few moments," Mr. Shaw grumbles, stepping into the open elevator. He adjusts his jacket and then is on his phone without giving me another glance.

I watch it close before I walk through the glass doors and then toward my desk. All the while my thoughts are on that exchange. Nothing seemed to give his feelings away one way or another, leaving me with a world full of confusion and another full day of anxiety.

"You didn't come here to catch a man," I mutter out loud, thanking my lucky stars it's only the two of us on this floor. Slipping off my coat and matching hat and glove set, I hang them in the coat closet and then return to my desk.

I get to work on the list of emails and notes he's left for me on my blotter. It's not too complicated and thankfully, I don't have any questions before he returns. I've only checked off two things on my list when he comes back with something that smells fantastic. I try to ignore the hunger pangs and work, keeping my head down so he doesn't think I'm focused on him.

His footsteps get closer and closer until they stop in front of my desk. I look up and see him staring at me for a moment. "I have two calls I'll be on today.

Also I have dinner with my sister tonight, so if you could remind me that I need to leave on time. I'd appreciate it."

"Yes, Mr. Shaw." He walks toward his office, face flat, hiding any kind of emotion, leaving me with nothing to judge.

For the rest of the morning, he stays in his office and then it's lunch time. Since he doesn't have a meeting on his calendar, I knock on his door. "Come in, Miss Novak."

"I'm going to head to lunch. Do you need anything before I go?" I can't read the expression that comes over his face as I wait for him to respond, but he looks fierce, dark, feral.

"No, Miss Novak."

"Okay. Should I start filing when I come back?"

"That would be good," he grunts, returning his attention back to his computer, effectively dismissing me. I quietly walk out and close the door behind me before grabbing my bag and head down to grab my lunch.

I hit up the restaurant in the lobby and get in line. Today's special is a burger bar, so I place an order for a medium well one with cheese. I turn and nearly collide right into Elliot who's almost standing on top of me. "Wow, it's good to see you're allowed to eat without the boss breathing down your back."

I take a step back. "I hardly see him, but it's only been two days."

"Well, it's cool. You can eat with us at our table. A bunch of us sit together at this time. Although a lot of people bring their lunch." He points to a group of people who are entering the elevator.

"I didn't know what we were doing today, so I decided to wing it for now. Maybe next week when I get the hang of things, I'll bring my lunch because I can't afford to be eating out every day or I'll have to actually exercise."

"You don't exercise? Damn, that's unbelievable."

"Well I don't do it for weight loss so it's just enough to stay active."

We get our food and Elliot tries to pay, but I don't want to give him the wrong idea. I'm not interested in dating him even if he's probably a better fit than a man like Jack Shaw.

The trip back to the lunchroom on the fourth floor is quick, so I have plenty of time to eat my lunch.

"This is Petra, she's Mr. Shaw's new assistant," he says.

A pretty, petite woman in her forties stands up and shakes my hand. "Oh wow. You're gorgeous. I'm

Sally by the way. I work in communications and development."

"I'm Will, and I work next to Sally, but I'm in IT, so if you have any tech issues you can give me a call." He nods his head in the middle of taking the lid off his food.

"I will."

"I'll handle all of the support requests for my office," Mr. Shaw snarls behind me. *Shit. Okay.*

"Miss Novak, I need to see you." I look down at my lunch like I didn't pay all this money for it to get cold. "Take your lunch with you," he grumbles when he reads my expression.

"Well, maybe another day." I wave bye to the crowd.

A low growl comes from Mr. Shaw. "Now, Miss Novak." I stand with my bag of food and he walks behind me out of the lunchroom like a punished child and I don't know what I did wrong.

We barely get to the elevator before he starts grumbling his complaints. "I'm already late because you forgot to submit the documentation to Mr. Redding for my meeting." I gasp because I was sure I hit send on the materials two hours ago.

"I'm sure I did it," I insist.

"He says he didn't receive it and now I have to

calm that bastard down." The doors to the elevator open and he helps me in. The second the doors close, he snarls, "What the fuck did I say about lunch with Elliot?"

"We met in line at the restaurant. Why does it matter anyway?" I challenged, looking up at him with a bit of irritation.

"I already explained that I don't want my assistant getting it on with the other staff members."

"Does this have to do with your last assistant?" I naturally look down at his crotch without thinking.

"No, this has to do with getting the job done properly. If you weren't so eager to get out of here to see Elliot you would have done your job right."

"I sent it to him," I hiss, stepping out of the elevator as soon as the doors open enough for me to get my body through them. I'm at my desk without looking back at him and I pull up my sent files. Turning my screen around, I point. "Look right there. Ten twenty-two. Sent," I punctuate for emphasis.

"Fine. Maybe it went to his spam. Eat your lunch there."

"An apology would be nice."

"When I don't have to reprimand you every day I'll be nice."

He starts to walk away to his office like he didn't just ruin my lunch. "Jerk," I mutter under my breath.

He whips his head around. "I'm a jerk, but I'm not deaf Miss Novak. Be careful, you're on thin ice."

Shit.

CHAPTER
Six

JACK

The second I'm in my office, I loosen my tie and take a deep breath. I wanted to smash Elliot's head into the table for fucking sitting so close to her. His chair had been much closer than everyone else's had been. I'm tempted to close the lunchroom for renovations and making stationary seats.

Since I met Petra, I can't fight the growing jealousy living in my veins. Pacing for a minute or two, I finally calm down enough to sit down and fix the lie I set up to retrieve her.

I message Petra and tell her that he found the documents and that I rescheduled the meeting for tomorrow at one. It's all bullshit because the second she walked out of the room, I called Redding and informed him that I needed to cancel the meeting.

The image of her meeting any of the other men in the building flooded my brain. There are several handsome bastards roaming the area who would gladly ask her out without a hint of hesitation. They're not her boss, so they don't have a fucking conflict blocking their path to happiness with her.

I'll fucking step in the way every time, but now it probably looks like I was into my last assistant too. Petra's the only one I want and I want her to stay away from Elliot who clearly is after her.

The prick has a problem if he thinks I'm going to let him get near her again. I'm about to fire his ass, but I need a legitimate reason for it. It's not like he's done anything wrong as far as the rules go but that doesn't mean I don't want to beat the shit out of him for trying to scoop Petra from under my nose.

A call comes in from human resources. "Hello, Ms. Hoffman. What can I do for you?"

"I need to make sure everything is well."

"What is the matter?" This is my company, so she better not be giving me shit.

"Nothing, I just saw you huffing into the lunchroom and by the time I was done speaking with an employee you were gone and they said you were upset with your new assistant. Does she need to be replaced?"

"No, it was a computer glitch on my client's end. Everything is fine. Miss Novak did her job and it was a miscommunication about the schedule."

"Okay. I just want to make sure we don't have a repeat of what happened a few months back, so if you want to fire her let me handle it."

"It won't be necessary."

Suddenly, I hear her delicate knock on the door and my cock stiffens. It doesn't matter that she's not in front of me yet. Just the thought of seeing her sends my arousal into overdrive. I end the call with HR because my moments alone with Petra need to be just that—only us two.

"Come in." My voice is gruff, thick with need and frustration.

"I wondered if you wanted me to start the filing now." Fuck me. Was her outfit that tight this whole time? It's no wonder why they're all eager to be by her. She's a goddess, but I'm going to covet her for myself.

"Yes, you could get started." I look at my watch and realize that she's only been at lunch for twenty minutes. "No, actually you haven't taken your full lunch, Miss Novak."

"I don't really need to. It's not like I have anyone to talk to out there at my desk. Besides, looking for another job on the company computer is frowned upon." She isn't going to find another job if I have any say in the matter.

"I'll have to agree with you on that. Come over here and get started." She nervously smiles at me when I give her one of my own. Fuck, I'm lost. How am I going to make a move when I don't know where to begin?

"So how many more do you have?"

"That stack over there and we should be caught up." I point to a decent pile stacked onto a chair next to the filing cabinet.

"Okay. She sashays over to the pile in the corner, passing by my desk in her form-fitting skirt. Biting back a groan, I want to push it up to her waist and run my hands and mouth all over her pussy and ass.

If she had any idea what I wanted to do to her she'd run away fast as hell. I'm acting like a sick fucker and I need to calm my ass down before I get out of control especially after everything that happened yesterday.

I try to focus on my work for the next hour as she files away all the documents. Our time is up when the phone rings. "Mr. Shaw's office. One moment please." She puts it on hold and looks up at me. "Marilyn is calling for you."

"I'll take this."

"Okay. I'll be at my desk." She leaves the room and I feel like I've missed something.

"Hey brat. What's going on?"

"Are we still on for tonight?" she asks, making me wonder what's going on underneath all that dark hair of hers. I've confirmed that with her this morning.

"I promised you."

"Yes, but you're usually working long hours." She has a point.

"I am, but I'll be cutting back soon after I find a few people to take the load off. Anyway, is that why you called?"

"Yeah, well, I wanted to just meet you at your office." A sinking suspicion is playing in my head. I want to tell her to stay away from Petra until I make headway with her, but I might need a middle woman.

"That is a great idea."

"Cool. I'll be down in two hours."

"Is it that late already?"

"Nope, but I have time to kill after my classes. Sorry not sorry." She hangs up on me because her motive is clear. She wants to meet Petra. I knew she wasn't satisfied with my explanation yesterday.

Checking my watch, it's time for my next meeting, so I get on my conference call which lasts nearly two hours. When I finally get off the phone, I go to step out and warn Petra about my sister, but I'm too late.

"Marilyn, are you harassing my assistant?" I growl, staring at my two favorite women in the whole world.

"I'm not the one giving her a hard time. Right, Petra?" Marilyn glares at me before winking at Petra.

"No, your sister's a sweetheart." She smiles at her and it's a genuine one that makes me think they'll be good friends. Maybe it's an excellent idea that she's here to help me smooth things over with Petra.

"I still have another hour."

"It's cool. I have a new book to read. Besides, I can teach your assistant all the fun ways to annoy you."

"Whatever she says…it's a lie." I wink at her and then head back to my office before I end up pulling her in my arms.

Working gets difficult when I know that my two favorite women are out there talking. I decide to take some work home because I can't concentrate and I need to get Marilyn away from her before she goes too far and scares her off by telling her that I've never gone out of my way for any of my employees like ordering her special outerwear.

After I pack up my things, I swing my coat on and hurriedly make my way out to find my sister missing and Petra at her desk working. "Where's my sister?"

"Ladies room."

"Oh, okay, thank you. You can pack up and go home. We're calling it a day early."

"Thanks."

I check my watch twice as I do my best not to beg her to join us. She slips on her coat and hat, scarf, and gloves. "Those look good on you," I blurt out the truth.

"Thank you," she blushes and I move a step closer, forgetting myself. I'm inches from her desk when I hear a cough.

"Are you ready, Jack?"

I whip my head around and step back from my assistant. "Yes. I've got work to handle when I drop you off, so I can get the rest done later."

"Well, it's been a pleasure to meet you, Petra. I hope to see more of you." We all take the elevator down even though we're going to the underground parking garage. Just as Petra exits at the lobby, my sister calls out, "By the way, I'd lose the boyfriend. Long distance relationships aren't great." She waves as the doors close, but I feel like I've been decked in the gut.

"What the fuck do you mean she has a boyfriend?" I snarl, ready to beat the fuck out of someone.

"How could she be that beautiful and still single? Just because you're picky doesn't mean everyone else is."

"Who is this boyfriend?" I want answers.

Marilyn shrugs as if my life isn't hanging on her every damn word. "I don't know. We didn't talk about him other than he lives in the suburbs so she only sees him on the weekend."

"We'll see about that." We walk into the parking garage and toward my vehicle.

"Why do you care, big bro? She's only your assistant." I snarl at her while she giggles, enjoying my anguish.

"I think it's a sushi night," I say, knowing Marilyn hates sushi.

She gasps and stops walking outside my sedan. "Don't be a jerk. Just work harder and maybe not be mean to the girl. She's under the impression that she's going to be fired at any moment."

"I'll work on it and she's going to get rid of that boyfriend." *Or I will.*

"Good, because you're not the only one interested."

It's my turn to freeze and look shocked. "You think?"

"Yes. Now, actually, let's hit up the hot dog stand by my house and then you can go home and think about your future. I can tell you're going to be shit company and I have a paper to write."

"So you only set this up because of Petra."

"Damn right." She winks and nudges my shoulder. I take her to our favorite little spot near her place. We get some greasy fast food and attempt to talk about school, but all I can think about is Petra and this boyfriend, so we finish the food quickly.

"I'm sorry I wasn't better company, Mare."

"I want you happy, so don't screw this up." She kisses my cheek as I drop her off at her apartment. Now it's time to learn to smooth things over with my future wife and make her lose the boyfriend.

As I drive to my condo, I think about my plans this week. "She won't be seeing him this weekend," I mutter to myself, smirking because I'll keep her very busy and thousands of miles away.

JACK

Five whole days. Hell, this is only the fifth day.

Every day, it's getting harder and harder to I wait for her to arrive at the office. It's like a kid waiting for presents at Christmas; I'm anxious and greedy as fuck.

It's been twelve hours since I've seen her, and twelve hours since I've gotten my fix of Petra Novak. How the fuck am I supposed to pretend that this is just a simple work relationship when all I want to do is dip into her pussy and make my fucking sons and daughters, tying her to me for life?

I've given up the pretense that my feelings are

that of boss and employee. My fascination with Petra has only grown with every passing day. She shines even when I give her shit for nothing. In fact, she tosses my attitude back at me, putting me in my place and I want to go caveman on her.

The guard I hired to keep an eye on Petra doesn't start until today. She won't be ready until Petra leaves the office because it was last minute and Landon had to find the right female guard for me to use, but all of her tracking devices have been activated for the past work week, and I know she's about two minutes away from the building.

I've been obsessed with Petra for an entire work week, and every single day it gets harder and harder to let her leave the office without me. Still, I drive to her apartment and check in to make sure she's home safe even though her devices say she is. I watch her walk sometimes.

Maybe I should have a car service take her home or get her an apartment close to the office. Better yet, she could move in with me. No, that's a terrible idea unless I plan to keep her tied to my bed for the foreseeable future. That's actually not a terrible idea at all.

My eyes are glued to the cameras watching the

doorway for her entrance and then my elbow nudges my coffee cup, sending it careening to the floor. Luckily it has a lid and the fucker is cold. I turn to pick it up and quickly get back to the screen, but I don't see her. Did she stop somewhere?

I check my phone, and she's in the building. Damn it, I missed what she's wearing. I didn't get a chance to see her as she walked in and see if she was happy to be here or if she had her gloves on. I stand up and walk out toward her desk and wait for the elevators to ding so I can see her arrive.

Time seems to move in slow motion as I stand there like a fool. After a minute, I grow impatient so I check her tracking device and see that she's still down in the lobby. "What the fuck is going on?"

She should have been up here by now. "Mr. Shaw?" I nearly jump out of my skin.

"Petra," I shout. "What are you doing up here?"

"I work here, but I have to run back down. I think I left my bag downstairs, or I hope I did."

"How could you leave your bag in the lobby?" I nearly bark out, but I catch my tone at the end.

"I was signing for a package and it was getting in my way."

"That's what security is for."

"Sorry."

"I'll go with you."

"You don't have to do that."

Tension fills me and I can't explain how irritated I am or even why. "I said I'll go with you, Miss Novak."

"I like when you call me Petra."

"Come on, let's go. I have meetings throughout the day."

"You have a lot of meetings. Do you ever get anything else done?" she blurts out, pressing her hand to her mouth.

I smile, trying not to laugh at the fact that she doesn't have much of a filter at all. "That's the point. Everything else gets pushed off to others. I make and close deals, handle a lot of details of what goes on with the company, while others handle what happens inside the company."

The elevator door opens, and we step inside. "I see. I really don't understand all of it, but I suppose that's why you're the boss and I'm a temp," she says as she presses the button and then the door closes, leaving us both together for a brief trip down.

"It takes time to understand the ins and outs of most companies. Mine holds stakes in different areas of manufacturing. We have fourteen different production lines in five different states and two different countries. We own produce and textiles, and I need to make sure that I'm negotiating with the proper channels to keep everything running smoothly for the future of the company and any family that I have."

"Do you have a family?" I can't gauge her feelings with that question, but I answer honestly because I have nothing to hide.

Looking into her pretty eyes, I say, "Not a wife and kids yet, but you met my younger sister. She can be a pain in the ass." I wink and she smiles. I want to know more about my woman, so I ask her the same question. "Do you, Petra?"

"Nope. It's just my roommate and me. My parents left me to the system when I was four." What pieces of shit could leave such a beautiful little girl?

"I'm sorry about that. So you have a roommate?" I'm about to question her when the elevator stops on the fourth floor and Elliot comes in with his cart. I swiftly hook my arm around Petra and pull her to the side so he doesn't bump her and quickly let her go so it doesn't appear improper even though that slight touch is seared into my skin through our layers.

"Sorry," Elliot mutters.

"It's okay. I wasn't paying attention," she says,

covering for the fact that I was being a bit overprotective.

A grin shoots over his young and handsome face. "So, how about I make it up to you with dinner tonight?" This fucker doesn't quit, and my temper grows hotter by the second.

"I can't. I'm going out with a friend." A friend? She doesn't mention that it's a boyfriend, maybe because she likes Elliot.

"Elliot, stop trying to hook up on company time." Although I say it calmly, the tension radiates through my body, and I'm sure they both can sense it.

He throws his hands up and steps slightly back. "I'm just apologizing, sir."

"Well, stop it before you're reported for harassment." Petra wisely stays silent and bites down on that bottom lip while two dogs fight over her like the last bone.

"Yes, sir," Elliot chokes out. We let him exit first because the cart's large and in the way. Also I don't want him to get a glimpse of her ass in her tight skirt.

I can't handle the rage burning in my gut at the way he was interested in her. She's mine, even if I can't claim her just yet. She belongs with me, but it's complicated. I wanted to kill Dickerson, and that's no fucking joke. The thought of ending the bastard still runs in my head after everything that happened last week.

She's not ready for what I have planned for us. One day I'll find a way to make her mine, but until that time, I'll have to keep all these other assholes away from her. She's like a magnet for horny men.

CHAPTER
Eight

PETRA

I swear he looks like he's going to snap the waiter's neck. "Mr. Shaw, are you okay?"

"I'm fine. Please call me Jack. After all, I'm calling you Petra." There's something sensual in the way he says my name that drives me to find reasons for him to call out for me.

"But you're the boss," I remind him, taking a drink of my water while I try to figure out what his intentions are.

"As long as you remember that," he says in a tone that makes me think he's not talking about work. My thighs clench together, and I imagine him telling me what to do as he pulls my hair and kisses me hard before demanding I bend over his desk.

Heat floods my face so I tilt my head away, looking out toward the window just as a group of men in suits pass by and they notice me. One of them gives me a wink, earning a growl from Jack. *Oops.*

"You okay?" I ask him as I turn back to him. "You should take a drink of water to clear your throat. Are you getting sick?"

"Sick, all right," he grumbles. I try to bite back the smile because I know damn well it's not what's wrong.

"Mr. Shaw—"

"I told you to call me Jack." His jaw clenches and his eyes darken in irritation. Does he have any idea what he does when he gets all out of control like that? Probably not.

"Jack, you can't growl and bark at every man that gives me any attention. You're just my boss, not my boyfriend or husband."

"We're at a business lunch."

Two minutes ago the waiter asked me if I needed anything, giving me a smile in the process. It's not like the guy outright gave me his number or asked for mine. Granted, he did smile at me a lot more and hardly looked Jack's way, but that's probably because he looks like he's ready to kill anyone in a heartbeat.

"And we haven't discussed an ounce of business, Mr. Shaw. What is it that you wanted to go over?" I ask, trying to do something about this tension growing between him and every single man around. He's like a wild beast in a fancy suit.

It makes me want to crawl in his lap and see if he'll grunt and growl while he manhandles me, running his hands all over me. I flush as my pussy flutters with arousal. *Shit.*

I clench my thighs together for the hundredth time, grateful that we're sitting across from each other so he can't see or feel the effect he has on me. I have to be quiet or I'll it come off like I'm playing a rhythm under the table with my inner thighs clapping.

He takes a drink of water and then says, "We have a trip to Vegas this weekend until Tuesday, so I need you to be prepared. Only on Sunday evening will you have time off."

"Are you serious?" I look at him like he's crazy as hell.

"I'm always serious, Petra."

"Thanks for the heads-up."

"Why? It was on my calendar as a full conference,

which is listed as something you're supposed to attend. Do you have something to do?"

"Yes. I have a date," I blurt out without thinking. It's a lie, but I'm flustered and confused. How am I supposed to just go to Vegas with him?

"Break it." There's that snarl again. Is he jealous?

"What? No," I argue, taking a bite of my creamy mushroom and chicken rice.

"Yes."

"I can't," I insist, pushing him a bit more.

"If you want to keep your job, you'll break it."

What is wrong with me? Am I trying to get fired? "Fine." I pull out my phone and send a text to Val. ***Sorry, I have to cancel our date night for a work thing.***

Make it up to me later, babe, she replies like the wonderful bestie she is.

I reply, ***I will*** with a kiss emoji.

I'll thank her later. He leans over and sees my message, snarling but not saying anything as we finish our meal quickly.

For the rest of the day, our conversations are short and to the point. He isn't mean, but he's not as sociable. I wonder if I've pushed him too far with the whole fake boyfriend and if any interest he had is out the window.

"Why doesn't your boyfriend pick you up from work?" he questions because I know he's not the kind of guy that would let his woman take the train.

"He doesn't live in the city. We don't get to see each other often," I lie as I put my coat on because I've already dug my hole, and there's no sense in backing off now. I told his sister the same story because she started bombarding me with questions like I was in an interrogation, and it was the only thing I could come up with.

"Be ready to leave at ten in the morning. I'll be at your apartment to get you," he barks out, looking a bit agitated.

"Okay. Do you need the address?" I ask him, reaching over to my desk to grab the Post-It notes and a pen.

"No. Human Resources has all the information. Be ready—don't be playing in bed with your lover. I'm not going to wait around just so you can get him off." I'd love to get Jack off.

"Yes, Jack."

"Goodnight, Miss Novak." I can't hide the frown on my face when I hear him call me by my last name. I suppose we're back to last names.

The whole way home, I'm lost in thought and fear about what's going to happen while we're away. It's crazy, but I hope something gives one way or another —he either fires me, or begs me to be his. I'm just about to get off the train, and I nearly bump into a random guy.

I reach out and touch his shoulder quickly apologizing. "Sorry."

"Don't worry, beautiful. I'd love to bump into you anytime."

"Sorry. Excuse me."

"Wait, Chica. Come talk to me." He reaches out for me, but I manage to dodge his grasp.

"No, thanks."

I start walking along the platform, shaking my head. What is it with men that don't know how to take a hint or even a direct no? Granted, the one I want confuses me like crazy because he blows hot and cold. Jack doesn't want me dating the guys at work, and growls at any man that gives me an ounce of attention, but he doesn't seem to want me for himself.

Suddenly, I feel someone too close to me again. I spin around ready to hit him with my heavy purse, but he's instantly pulled away from me by a woman of all people. She looks tough and I swear I've seen her before.

"Leave her alone, or I'll make sure you'll never

be able to flirt with a woman again," she warns him with a violent calm in her voice that gets his attention.

The guy backs off and I silently thank her, making my way home faster than I ever have before. As I get to my building I see her not far behind. She stops just a few doors down and heads into an apartment building next door.

Could she just happen to work downtown too? It's a strange coincidence, but it's very possible, of course. So many people work downtown and travel from the southside. It's not unheard of to have a nine to six.

As soon as I slide the key is in the door, Val yanks it open. "Hey, Petra, so do you care to tell me what's up with that message?"

I take my key from the door and thankfully it isn't broken. Walking in, I shake my head and take off my hat and coat.

"Are you going to answer me?" She pesters me after closing the door.

"Yeah, so the boss man has me going to Vegas with him tomorrow." I go straight into my bedroom because there's just too much to do in a short time.

"Wait. So he didn't tell you this all week but decided to spring it on you today?"

"I know, right?"

"Let's look for the sexiest work clothes we can find. Maybe some nighttime outfits. You're going to be in Vegas, after all. He doesn't own all your time." She winks.

I'm going to be one of two things by the end of the weekend: unemployed, or defiled by my boss. I'm truly hoping for the latter. God, I'm craving the latter.

We spend the next two hours packing and snacking. Then I send him a text, asking if he needs me to bring anything in particular.

Just yourself.

I want to ask if clothing is optional, but that would be so wrong so instead, I just respond with a quick, **Okay.**

"Girl, you should have just asked if clothes were necessary."

"Yeah, so he could fire me before we go."

"He's not going to fire you. I think the guy wants to do you dirty, and I don't mean it in a bad way. He wants to fuck you until neither of you can see straight or walk at all."

"What makes you think that?" I ask her, needing reassurance.

"You might not have noticed, but how many times have you mentioned that he's there when you first walk into the office."

"Every morning."

"The guy actually waits by the elevator until you arrive." She's got a point, but he could just be arriving minutes before I do and it's a coincidence.

It does strike me that his coat and things are in his office already. She shakes her head like she's reading my thoughts. "He's like a puppy waiting for his owner to come home. I'm telling you—all you have to do is wear something sexy and flirt with any of the men at the conference, and he'll be carrying you out of that hall over his shoulder, ready to take you back to the room."

"Girl, please. I think you read too many romance books."

"I bet you twenty bucks."

"You're on."

"Petra, I was supposed to meet Mr. Wilbanks down there five minutes ago," Jack calls through the door, sounding more annoyed by the second.

"Go without me. I promise I'll be down there shortly. I can take the elevator by myself."

"Fine. Don't take too long, or I'll have to send a

search party for you," he growls, and then his strong footsteps make their way toward the door, leaving me in the hotel suite alone.

We have a two-bedroom suite that's the size of a large apartment for the entire weekend. It must cost a fortune, but I've learned that Mr. Shaw is more than rich; the man is wealthy.

Finally, I wait two more minutes and then grab my things. I'd been ready for twenty minutes, stalling because I didn't want him to tell me to change or disinvite me if he saw my outfit.

Most of the women here will be wearing something similar. In fact, I saw one of the ladies here earlier, and she was already dressed in a tiny cocktail dress that barely covered her ass.

Now that I think about it, I better hurry before they latch on to his side. What if Val's wrong and he's not interested in me like that?

Building up the bravery, I leave the room and take the elevator down to the lobby. "Hello, Miss. Can I help you?" I'm greeted by a man in a nice hotel issued suit. He clearly takes an interest in my looks but still keeps a professional distance. I'm sure it's normal to be surrounded by beautiful, half-clothed women all day in Vegas.

"I'm looking for the Business Expo drinks hour."

"Yes, down here in this hall." I follow him as he leads the way. The doors open, and I'm greeted by another gentleman in a matching uniform at a table with set of badges laid out.

"Hello, Ma'am. Your name?" he asks.

"Petra Novak with Shaw Enterprises." He continues to look at his list multiple times and then back up at me.

"Sorry, there must be a mix-up. We have you listed as Petra Shaw, Shaw Enterprises. We can have it fixed in the morning."

I flush with embarrassment. They hand me my lanyard. Damn it. I slide it over my neck but turn the name tag around so it's facing inward.

"There's no need to bother," Jack growls, turning my badge around. "It'll keep the perverts off my assistant." I blush deeper and duck my head as he presses his hand to the small of my back.

A woman in a nice red dress with a slit down her right leg appears, and I'm shocked at how beautiful she is. She smiles and says, "I doubt it will do much good because she's not wearing a ring and she's stunning, but who knows. Good luck. Maybe try wearing a potato sack. Then again, on you, dear, you'd probably still be stunning."

"Thank you," I answer. Although she's playing nice the look in her eyes reads pure viper.

"Yes. I'll look and check to see if we still make those burlap sacks," Jack mutters. "Excuse us."

We turn away from the table, and Jack is about to lead us toward the exit when an overweight-looking man with a full head of gray hair says, "Hello, Shaw. I'm glad you finally found me. At first, you were too busy with Miss Rice, but it seems you've brought your own little beauty with you. Petra Shaw?" So that woman is Miss Rice. I've heard her name mentioned in meetings and files. Her father owns a major company that works with Jack and I'm betting she has her eyes set on more than business with him.

"A mix-up with the name tags. I'm Petra Novak, his assistant." I wave my bare hand. "Happily not married, but I do have a boyfriend back in Chicago."

"It's a pity. I have a son somewhere around here who gets his genes from his mother's side. He could use a beauty like you on his arm," Mr. Wilbanks says, taking my hand and kissing the back of it. Jack yanks it back like a jealous husband and I want to smile, but I maintain my professionalism, and remember what Val said.

"Mr. Wilbanks, I believe you wanted to discuss a trade deal."

"Yes, please do talk. I'm about to get a drink." I step away from Jack and head straight to the bar. The drinks are linked to our ID cards, so I order a margarita and stand at the bar while I wait.

Turning back, I steal a look at Jack and the man. Jack has purposely turned his body to get a better view of the bar from here. His eyes are glued to me, watching intently with a mixture of lust and anger in those gorgeous eyes of his.

"So, you're here with Jack Shaw. That's a first that he'd bring his assistant on a trip, and how convenient of you to have your name tag botched. I know he's not married and I have my eyes set on him, so you can just find yourself another guy."

I see her lanyard reads April Rice, and I want to kick her. She's pretty, of course, with a killer body that men drool over, and like Wilbanks says, they were probably making plans to hook up later when I walked in.

"Good for you. It's nice to have plans. Although this one isn't up to just you, so I'd be careful what you say. My boss takes his reputation seriously, and if you're going to announce an engagement before he does, maybe you should let him know."

"We're not engaged, you little twit."

"Whatever, then get out of my way." I take my

drink and walk off toward the two men when a third joins, and he's handsome. Not as handsome as Jack Shaw, but then again, there aren't many men in the world that could rival Jack's looks.

As I reach them, Jack takes my drink and smells it before taking a sip. "This is pretty good. I'll have to get one of them instead of this shitty IPA."

"Seriously, it's one of the worst brands," the man I haven't been introduced to says. "I switched beers before I took a second drink, but what I really want to know is who are you, and will you marry me?" He bows his head slightly.

"Not unless you have a death wish," Jack states as a matter of fact.

"He's teasing. I'm his assistant, Petra, and you are?" I reply after taking a long drink of my margarita that I've taken back from my boss. I'm going to need it because both of these men actually seem serious.

"Enchanted. I'm Richard Wilbanks."

"Oh, yes. Your father said you were around here. I'm going to get another drink since someone drank half of mine. I'm here to have some fun while I'm in Vegas."

"I could show you a good time."

"Not if you end up in the hospital."

I give Jack a look of shock and then say, "Please

continue talking shop. Do you need me to get you anything, Mr. Shaw?"

He leans in, grips my arm with his thumb rubbing my elbow, and then whispers, "Mrs. Shaw, you and I will talk about this later." He straightens up. "Sorry, she is new and doesn't know much about the company yet."

I walk away, trying to avoid the squishy feeling between my thighs. I am grateful that my dress is black and the lights are low so no one can notice that my pussy is drenching my panties.

Jack is such a strait-laced, suit-wearing, dedicated CEO that hearing him growl when he speaks to me or about me sets my body ablaze. I want to come just hearing his voice. But the death blow was calling me, Mrs. Shaw.

I'm almost to the bar when I nearly bump into a man. "Oh, I'm sorry," I say, giving him an apologetic smile.

"Goodness, since when did they include models in these expos? Please tell me you're single." He looks down at my name tag, but he stops to linger too long at my chest and doesn't get that far. "You're hiding your name from me." I drop my head and realize my tag is twisted.

He reaches out to grab it, but before he can, a

strong hand grips his and yanks it away. "Baxter, keep your filthy eyes and hands off her."

"Mr. Shaw," I gasp. It's all I can say as my glass falls out of my hand and my body lands upside down over Jack's shoulder. His strong, thick arms flex around my thighs as he holds me firmly to his body. I'm shocked and a bit mortified, but I'm mostly aroused as I stare at his perfect ass and legs.

CHAPTER
Nine

JACK

"Put me down," she huffs, legs dangling as I carry her out of the cocktail hour. What the fuck was she thinking, wearing that? She has to know what she does to me by now.

"No. Stop struggling or you're going to fall or worse, show people your tight little pussy." I swat her ass, hearing the soft gasp as my hand makes contact with her round bottom.

"Well, no one would see my bottom if I wasn't upside down."

"You shouldn't be wearing this dress."

"It's Vegas, Mr. Shaw." I press the elevator button, and it opens immediately, making me grateful because I'm feeling heated and aroused at the same fucking time. I slide her down the front of my body and onto her feet. She adjusts the top of her dress because her breasts are almost popping out. I lick my finger and then run my finger over her cleavage.

"You're dressed like you're ready to be fucked," I grunt.

Her chest rises and falls as she attempts to catch her breath. Looking up at me, she attempts to glare, but she's so small that she's too adorable to be tough. "You know…I don't know what you're talking about. Everyone is dressed like this and I'm here to have a good time"

"Yes, and Wilbanks offered to show you a fucking good time." I wanted to choke the life out of him in an instant.

"He didn't say fucking. Besides, I have a boyfriend, in case you've forgotten." She poked her finger into my chest.

"Not any fucking more," I snarl, wanting to make her forget all about the bastard. I grab her hand, take the finger that she dared to poke me with, and suck it into my mouth. She lets out a gasp followed by a pretty moan. "You're mine," I growl, biting lightly before I let it go, cup the back of her neck and taste her lips for the first time.

A cough comes from the left. I pull back and see the door is open, and there's a group of people waiting to get on the elevator. "This is our floor," I state.

I look down to make sure her tits aren't showing before I drag her out. If any of these fuckers get a look, I'll dig their eyes out with my pen knife. The second we clear the elevator doors, I sweep her up into my arms and cradle her until we reach our suite. The thought of creating any distance between us after that amazing kiss is unbearable.

"Jack, what are you doing? I can walk."

"I need you to save your strength because tonight you'll be using it all while riding my cock." Petra blushes, but she doesn't argue with me, which is wise because I can feel the energy coming off her and she wants me to take her, boyfriend or not. The fucker doesn't even live in the same city. What kind of shitty boyfriend is that?

I tap my keycard on the door and tug the door handle, letting us inside the room with a push and kicking it closed once I clear the doorway.

The lights in the foyer are on a motion sensor and give a path toward the bedroom where I lead my lover. Tonight I will have her, and by morning she and I will be so sore and tired we'll forget all about the damn conference and I'll have her tied to me.

Fuck, maybe I'll ply her with enough drinks this weekend and slide her on through to one of those wedding chapels, getting a ring on her finger while putting my son in her belly. Fuck, my hard cock stiffens further, digging into her hip as I move toward the bed.

I lie her on the bed with her little black dress riding up so I can see her black lace panties and her bare pussy lips peeking through. Fuck me. I grip my dick, squeezing it to stave off the urge to nut right here. I've got a lot to do before I shoot off my load into her tight womb. "Damn, your cock is massive. You're going to tear me apart with that one," she says.

"Thanks, my pet. Good—I want you to forget about anyone else but me. I want you to feel every inch of me for the rest of our days."

She arches her brow, pouting her bright red lips at me that had men ready to drop to their knees downstairs. "Prove it, Mr. Shaw."

A growl rips from my chest as I hear her get formal with me. She's testing me, knowing that I prefer her to say my name. "You call me Mr. Shaw again, and I'm going to redden your ass."

I'm grateful that I chose to go without a tie and

suit jacket because I need less between us as soon as possible. Freeing my belt from its clasp, I pull it from the loops and bring the ends into one hand, snapping it together. "Do you want a spanking, my pet, or are you going to be a good girl?"

"I'll be a good girl…for now," she finishes as I toss the belt on the floor. I'd never hurt my precious woman, but I want to see the heat in her eyes. Fuck, they shine with lust so provocatively I want to drown in them.

"Such a fucking teasing sin, you are, Petra. You're going to get fucked so damn hard that you'll need some painkillers and some booze to soothe the pain of your aching muscles." I grip her ankles and spread her legs apart so I can fit right where I want to be. Grabbing the hem of her dress, I tug it up over her body, lifting the stretchy material that clings to her hourglass figure so perfectly.

"My pet, you're so precious. I want to lick every inch of you, and you're going to let me because you're mine."

"For tonight."

I brush my nose against hers and then look into her eyes. "You're mine forever. I'm not letting you go back to him. I'm putting my baby into you, breeding your pussy, filling your womb, and keeping you, even if that means tying you to my bed."

My hand skims down her side, thumb rubbing her breast and then turning it to cup her hip and then her ass, squeezing it and grinding our pelvises together. She hisses and moans when my slack-covered cock rubs against her heated pussy.

Her panting intensifies as I bring my mouth to her throat. "I need you, Petra. Tell me you're going to give me what I need."

"Take me, Jack. Make me come, please." I yank down her bra, needing to see more of her before I lose my mind. Her hands thrust into my short hair, tugging on the top as I suck on her plump tits, snagging her right nipple between my teeth while cupping and squeezing her left. Her areolas stiffen with my touch, becoming small and darkening to a berry color. Biting down, I feel her react to me, moaning, thighs clenching as her hips rock.

Every part of her body moves, itching for relief. "Jack."

"Yes, my pet?"

"I ache." Her voice is shaky, full of need.

"Let me take care of that." I slide down her smooth skin, kissing lovingly down her body as I make my way to her lace-covered pussy. My lips brush over the material before I swipe my tongue along the edge, causing her to shiver. Smiling against her mound, I revel in knowing that I can make her feel this way. Grabbing the edge of the lace, I give it a good yank and tear the material.

"Animal."

Looking up from the thin strip covering her tiny lower lips, I smile wickedly at my woman. "That I am. You've turned me into a fucking beast."

"So you don't normally growl all the time?"

"Only when men vie for your attention. It belongs to me." Pride wells in my chest when I press my finger past her folds and into her soaked depths. She's drenched for me as I press my tongue to her seam, licking her slit like ice cream.

Fuck, my ball sack lifts, tightening, readying to unload with every flick of my tongue lapping up her flavor. Curling my finger inside, I feel how fucking tight she is and know my dick is going to tear her pussy apart, marking her for me.

She'll definitely forget about that pencil dick. Maybe they just haven't fucked yet. Well, it's his motherfucking loss because there's no way she'll ever see him again. I'll kill the bastard first before I let her return to him. Not after she lets me have her sweet honey on my tongue and feel her warmth wrapped around me. God, I need to be inside her with my cock, breeding her. I can't let her leave me.

I've lost it. I'm obsessed. Out of my mind. Nuts. Still, Petra is mine, and by this weekend, she'll be my wife.

I'm doing my best to take my time because she's so fucking narrow that my finger's constricted and I can barely push a second one in to widen her up to take my huge cock. Turning my head to find my strength, I bite her thigh, making her moan my name. "Jack, take me."

"Your hole is too tight, my pet. I'm going to destroy it," I tell her, hoping Petra understands how much I'm thinking of her own well-being and that my restraint is only holding on by a thread.

"You've already destroyed me for anyone else." Those are all the words I need to hear. I rise up and stand on the side of the bed to quickly remove the rest of my clothes. With my length jutting out, I stroke it several times as I climb back onto the bed, my eyes focused on Petra and her reaction to me.

She licks her lips, and my cock nods in agreement with her silent request, but I can't. "Later," I whisper as she tries to lift to her knees. Nudging her back down, I brush my lips onto hers.

"Just a little lick," she whimpers as I lean down with my fingers rubbing her clit.

"So tempting. I can't wait to see your lips around my cock, sucking me down your throat. I've pictured you under my desk, blowing me while I sit in a meeting. Fuck, you have no idea how many times I've imagined bending you over my desk, drilling your pussy and then summoning Elliot into my office so he could see that you fucking belong to me, Petra. You're mine," I state, punctuating my statement with a possessive kiss before moving back to kneeling before my desire.

With my hands on her knees, I urge them apart, making room for me between her legs so I can see my glistening prize. She's shining for me, ready as she's gonna get for my massive length. I push my tip through her tiny entrance, watching it stretch her hole and disappear. I take a calming breath because she's so excruciatingly snug that I feel like I'm in a blissful grip of death. If this is the way to go, take me now.

My hands hold her thighs open wide so I can see myself sink in deeper, slowly pushing into her. Then I feel the slightest resistance, causing me to look up at my pet. Revealing her secret to me, giving me her gift, I selfishly steal it, opening it rapidly in one slam of my hips.

"You're all mine. Now breathe. I'm in you, Petra. That pussy belongs to me, so take a deep breath and relax because I'm going to make you feel really good soon, but first I need to see my reward." I feel animalistic as I lean back and see her blood on my cock. I swipe the blood off my length and rub it over my heart.

"Are you ready for me to breed you, Petra?"

"Yes, sir."

"I like that answer. I can't wait to have you in the office answering just like that while I fuck you on the conference room table. Do you want that?"

"Yes, Jack. I've wanted you to bend me over your desk so many times," she confesses. I'll make that shit a reality when we get back for sure.

"I will, but first it's time to fill your cunt with my sons. I need you dripping wet before I even let you think about leaving this bed."

"Fill me, Mr. Shaw." Growling, I pull out of her and flip her onto her stomach.

"Miss Novak, you're a bad girl." I swat her ass with my hand, watching it turn pink instantly. She yelps and then moans, rolling her hips back, looking for another. I give her two more on each side before dipping my head to eat her pussy some more. I want her wild for me. Tasting her cherry on my tongue, I feel like a fucking king after a long, victorious battle.

With another bite to her ass, I rise up behind her and nudge her knees apart with mine. "Time to finish what we started, Miss Novak. Although we're going to have to fix your name soon."

"Oh yeah?"

"Yes. You'll be Mrs. Shaw," I grunt, slamming into her.

She gasps from the depth of my entry, gripping the headboard. "Fuck, you're so deep."

"Good. You need to be punished, Petra. You've been keeping this pussy away from me. You should have been sitting on my desk the moment you walked into my building, spreading your legs out wide and giving me a taste of my favorite treat. A whole week of torture. A week of beating off—to thoughts of claiming that pussy."

She arches her back and turns her head with a smile. "You should have taken it, Mr. Shaw. I've been waiting for you to get so fed up with me and teach me to be a better assistant," she pants. I pump into her, driving deep with every stroke.

"You're the best assistant, but you're going to make a much better wife and mother," I grunt, pinching her nipples. She cries out, coming on the spot, clenching her tight sheath around my length.

With a roar, I shoot my seed. "See that I'm filling you up, my pet. Take my seed."

"Give it to me," she demands as she bounces her ass back on my cock, taking me. Sweat beads down my back as I lean over her body, trying to catch my breath. I pepper kisses up her spine until I reach her throat, licking her pulse.

"Marry me."

"Yes, sir."

PETRA

I take another shot in the back of the limo. I can't believe Jack talked me into a drive-thru wedding. I'm giggling in an all-white slip of a gown, straddling his lap while we wait.

This night has been insane. I can't believe I came out of the room wearing the dress that Val picked out. It was clearly a size too small for my breasts, making them look larger than they were; granted, I'd been blessed with D-sized boobs on a small frame.

Now my large chest is in his face and Jack's hands are gripping my round bottom, squeezing my meaty flesh. I've downed two more shots in the limo, feeling nervous about this whole thing. Has he lost his mind about marrying me because he took my virginity?

"Are you marrying me because you took my virginity, Mr. Shaw?"

A fresh smack on my ass is my answer. "Woman, what did I say? You're mine. You've been mine from the moment I caught sight of you, and you'll be mine until the day they put us in the fucking ground. I'm not kidding. Virginity or not, drunk or not, you're going to truly be Mrs. Shaw as soon as we get through this line, which doesn't seem to want to move, but that's just fine because I have a lesson to teach your pretty ass."

"What lesson would that be, Jack?"

"You make me so horny that I need you all the time. Including right now." He frees himself from his slacks and then lifts my dress, pulling my panties to the side. "Rub your pussy on my cock and get him nice and hard so I can fuck that tight cunt."

"I have a much better idea." I slide off his lap and onto the floorboard of the limo.

"Take him into your mouth. Suck my cock."

"Yes, sir." His dick jerks, and it arouses me the way I have control over his body. There are no lasting scars from the coffee burns from that bitch, and his cock is so fucking pretty, smooth and hard with just the right amount of veins that make me want to worship it. I've never done this before, but I want to please him. I've imagined sliding under his desk and undoing his pants, so I take that and use it as my game plan.

I run my hand up and down his shaft, slow and steady at first, learning the feel of his length. It gets heavier with every stroke and a bead of clear pre-cum forms at the tip. My mouth salivates, so I swipe my tongue over my bottom lip before I lower my head. Slurping on his tip, I get my first taste of his huge meat.

A deep groan rips from his throat and then I feel his hand grip the back of my head. "My pet, fuck, you're going to make me come down that pretty throat." I move up and down, faster and faster, loving how good it feels in my mouth while he tugs on my hair.

A moan comes from me as I pull off to breathe, but it's short lived because I need more. I want Jack's dick in my mouth. I'm so fucking horny that my knees slide apart and I clench my pussy. Taking my hand off his length, I move it over my body, squeezing my breasts, pulling down the left strap of my dress so my boob is freed. Pinching my nipple and playing with it, I continue to tease myself while sucking on him. He growls and reaches around to grab my tit as well.

"Fuck, are you turned on while sucking on my cock?" he asks as he yanks my head back.

"Yes," I pant, dribble on my lips as I pull off the tip.

"Climb up and ride me. I want that tight, soaked snatch impaled on my thick motherfucking cock." He lifts me before I can help myself, sucking my freed breast into his mouth on the way. "Sorry, that baby was in my face," he says as he adjusts me on his lap. I straddle him and move my panties to the side as he guides the tip to my entrance. "Slide down and work my pole."

"Fuck, it's so big."

"It's your doing. It's all for you, my pet. Ride me and fucking take my seed." He cups the back of my head under my hair and brings my face to his, kissing me hard.

I moan around his mouth, whimpering his name between our tongues dancing and his hips driving into me.

"Ride." I bounce on him, taking his length in short, fast movements as I get closer and closer to coming. My heart's pounding out of my chest as I cry out my orgasm and feel his cum shoot into my depths.

Then I feel the jolt of the vehicle coming to a stop. "Sir, we're up."

"Oh my goodness."

"Cover your tits." I'm already doing it as he says it. He pulls me off him long enough to zip himself, but that's it. I'm back on his lap and we're sitting by the door when he lowers the window and the officiant is there to get our information and have the ceremony begin.

I'm flush and sweaty from being thoroughly fucked and I'm sure he can smell the fact that we just had sex, but he politely smiles and does his thing.

By the time he pronounces us husband and wife, he adds, "Don't fret, my dear. You would not be the first couple caught up in passion by the time you reached the drive-up window."

"Thank you."

"Congratulations, Mr. and Mrs. Shaw." The man gives us the final documents that are signed by their notary and we drive back to the hotel.

"I can't believe we're married," I sigh before a sleepy yawn comes from me.

"Neither can I."

It's so freaking early when I wake up with a heavy ring on my finger.

Jack and I are married.

Blaming the alcohol is pointless because I know it's not the truth and it's what I wanted. I look over to where he's sleeping after our night together. It's only seven in the morning, but I need some air and time to think. I forced him to react; will he feel trapped when he learns there's no one else? Has he figured out that I lied about the boyfriend?

I shoot Val a text even though I know she's probably still sleeping. She has a big day tomorrow for her new job. She's probably going to want to know how my night went, so I send her a quick text that I'll try to call later because I don't have time to explain that I married him.

She's going to be pissed when she finds out that she missed the wedding. Although, I'm glad no one else saw it. I blush, thinking about getting caught up so much that I didn't feel the car move up in the line.

We need to talk tonight. Miss you.

I need some coffee, so I get dressed because I don't want to order up room service in case Jack has plans. I'll just run down to the café and come back. Grabbing my wallet out of my purse, I leave the room and head downstairs.

Goodness, the line is long at this time. "You're up early this morning. You must have had an early night," Mr. Wilbanks says with a smirk.

"Actually, I didn't, but I'm not sure that matters. I hope you rested up. It's going to be a busy conference tomorrow."

"I am. Although, my son was serious about his offer. If you still want to join us for breakfast, we'd love to have you over at our table."

"Thank you, but Jack wouldn't like that."

"He's only your boss. I get that he's a bit of a caveman, but we all know he was out with that other woman last night. The one in the red dress."

"Miss Rice?" I ask, wanting to laugh.

"Yes, I saw them leaving personally last night."

"Do me a favor and shut your filthy mouth. I don't know what deal you had with Jack, but I'm going to make sure it doesn't happen. You have to be a fool to think that he'd leave our bed last night to run off with her."

"You're a fool to think a man like him would be faithful to a simple assistant. He's going to just fire you like the rest of his assistants."

"Don't try that with me. It's not going to work."

"What's that?" He gestures toward my hand.

"Oh, this?" I wave my hand in his face. "These?

My wedding rings. Jack and I got married last night, so I know damn well he wasn't with anyone else. Now leave me alone. Great. The line is longer." I storm out of the hotel, deciding to find another place to get a coffee and get away from this jerk.

I try not to think about what he said. I know that Jack didn't screw his assistants, but I can't shake the silly jealousy. I find a coffee shop and pick up an iced coffee and a donut because I need some food in me. I'm starving and really want something hearty, but I'll have to wait for Jack. I need to be heading back.

When I get back inside the hotel, I remember that I forgot to take a key card. Great. I decide to sit in the lobby and hope Jack comes looking for me.

Eleven

JACK

"Where the fuck is she?" I snarl, waking up to my wife completely missing. Storming around the suite, I can't find her anywhere. Panic sets in and I look for her trackers on her phone, but it says she's in the suite. Fuck, her phone is right here along with her purse, but her wallet's gone. I call Carla, her bodyguard.

"Carla, where the fuck are you?" I bark into the phone.

"Following your wife. She left early this morning with her wallet. She's shopping in the store down in the lobby."

"Oh. Okay. Keep an eye on her. I'll be right

down." I look at the clock and realize it's already ten on Sunday. I slept half the morning away, but she didn't bother to wake me up before cutting out. Why didn't she take her phone or anything?

"That woman is going to get it the second I get my hands on her for leaving our bed." Her phone beeps, and it's a message from someone named Val. I open the message and I see the text exchange from the other day and the new messages between them. This must be the ex.

We need to talk tonight. Miss you.

Okay. Miss you too.

No, the fuck you won't be talking to this asshole. I dial the number, and a woman answers. "Hey, girl, please give me all the details with the hot boss. Did he drag you off to get married?"

"Details? Where the fuck is her ex-boyfriend?"

"Oh shit. Why do you have Petra's phone?"

"My wife forgot it, and let's just say I wanted to end their relationship for her."

"I knew it," Val squeals.

"Knew what?" I ask.

"You would find a chance to marry her in Vegas. She doesn't have a boyfriend, but if you hurt my best friend, I'll find a way to destroy you, Jack-ass."

"She doesn't have a boyfriend, even that ex?"

"Nope. I knew you wanted my bestie. Petra didn't believe me." *How could she not see how much I wanted her?* "I figured it wouldn't be a big deal if she had a fake boyfriend. It wards guys off and makes the right one work for it."

"Well, she's taken. Now I need to find her ass because she forgot her phone in the room. Just so you know, she'll be busy for the rest of the day. Too busy to be calling. Maybe after she's well rested she'll give you all—well, most—of the details on her hot boss." I end the call, grinning from ear to ear.

I leave the room with my wife's phone in my pocket because I'm going to have some fun with her ass for making me a jealous fucking mess, but first, I need to kiss the hell out of her. It's been hours since I've had my mouth on her and I need my fix.

When I finally get to the lobby, I see the younger Wilbanks on the ground holding his balls and Carla protecting Petra. Shit, my secret's out in the open too.

"What the fuck is going on here?" I snarl, grabbing Petra and wrapping my arms around her to protect her.

Carla's the first to speak. "He got a little too fresh. He thought he could pull the moves on her. She kicked him in the nuts, and then I shot him with my taser."

"Good. I ought to kill you myself for putting your hands on my wife," I snarl down at the pathetic bastard.

"Do you care to explain who she is and why I see her everywhere I go? I thought it was a coincidence by my apartment, but this is too much." I believe she already knows the answer, but she wants my reasoning.

"I've hired her to protect you when I'm not around."

"Really?"

"Yes."

"God, I love you." I expected her to be mad, so I was floored and pleased with her reaction. She throws her arms around me and we kiss wildly. I grip her ass and carry her back toward the elevators. I pull my lips away long enough to tell Carla to deal with this asshole and get back to me later.

"Yes, Mr. Shaw."

"Come, wife. I have to show you how much trouble you're in for leaving our bed this morning and messaging your ex."

"Oh…about that." I crush my mouth to hers to stop her from explaining. No, I want her right where I have her so I can fuck the hell out of her before I reveal I'm aware of her scheme to see if I wanted her. God, how could she have not seen it?

Linda in HR mentioned it to me yesterday, suggesting I be careful or I could have a lawsuit on my hands. She had no idea what lengths I'd go to get Petra, and a lawsuit would be the last of my concerns because I'm pretty sure kidnapping is a felony.

As soon as I get her in the room, I strip her out of her tee shirt and bra. "These tits are so full and sexy. I can't get enough of them." I sit her on the large foyer table and lean her back to get better access to them. My mouth moves from left to right and then back, sucking and nipping on the tenderness of her flesh, marking it with mini love bites.

"You're mine, Petra. What the fuck did you think you were doing leaving me all alone this morning?" I cup her sex through her beige capris, my thumb rubbing her bundle of nerves through the layer of clothes until I have her legs shaking.

"I couldn't sleep, but you looked so peaceful sleeping and I wanted some coffee. I was going to come right back but I forgot my keycard."

"You could have knocked on the door, asked the front desk for a second card." I grip her ass, squeezing it hard, rocking myself against her mound while I scold my wife.

"I didn't want to be a hassle."

"Wife, I want you wrapped up in my arms when I wake up. Hassle my ass, okay?"

"Okay."

"Good, now it's time to remind you who you belong to because you're over here talking about calling your ex while you're married to me, and that shit isn't cool at all. Fucking telling the bastard how much you missed him? Do you think that's acceptable, my pet?"

"No…but…"

"Did you just try to qualify your fuckup?" I crush her mouth to mine because I'm so full of shit and I want to fuck her good and hard. "You're mine."

I grab the button to her pants and pop it open, sliding them down with her panties while removing her sandals at the same time. I want her ass completely naked.

She's so fucking sexy sitting on the marble surface bared to me. I yank her thighs wide open, lift my tee shirt over my chest, and then drop to my knees. I have to eat her pussy. It's been hours since I've had her tight little hole in my face, and I want it so badly. It should have been my breakfast first thing when I woke up.

"Time to have my breakfast." I swipe my tongue

along her seam, and it parts slightly as I lick her sticky crème off her lips. My dick slams against my zipper, beating on it, ready to bust out of its cage, but I have to get my woman ready because I'll unload too quickly. Her pussy's a little too puffy after all the fucking we've been doing, but I'll get her ready to take my cock. I shove one digit into her hole, letting her wetness help open her up for my meat.

"I need your big cock inside me. Fuck, I want to be brutalized, Mr. Shaw," she shouts. Fuck.

"And you are. You're a bad girl." Pumping two fingers into her hole double time until she's squirming, I pull them out, turn her onto her belly, and stand behind her. Freeing my cock with one hand, I use my pussy-soaked fingers to tease her asshole. "This is mine too. I should fuck this hole too. Would you let me take your ass, my pet?"

"If that's what you want."

"I want whatever you give me." I push a finger inside just a bit. I don't want to hurt her, and as horny as we both are, I know there's no way in hell we're ready for that. I shove my cock into her pussy while my finger works her ass in and out. "Jack," she whimpers, popping her ass back and trying to get more of me inside her.

"Take it easy, babe. I don't want to hurt you."

Fisting her hair, I use it to drive my dick inside her cunt as she presses her hands on the table. "You look so hot spread out like this."

I lift her up a little more, putting her whole body onto the table, knees out wide so her pussy's nearly flush with the surface but almost completely off the edge and ass up in the air as I pound her from this angle.

"God, you have no idea how much I want to just own your entire body. Fucking you like this makes me want to drive into you on every surface in every different way." I lean over her as my cock pistons into her and my finger dips deeper into her ass. She gasps as her orgasm builds, walls clenching around my shaft.

I could nut right on the spot, but I keep my pace steady and breathe against her neck words of devotion and promises of the future. "I can't wait to breed this little pussy and fill you up with my babies, Petra. You're going to give me a family."

"I'm not on birth control."

"That's fucking good because I'm going to make sure you're getting stuffed every single day."

"Fuck, I'm coming, Jack."

"That's it; squeeze all that seed out of me. Time to make some baby Jacks." My legs shake as I finally stop coming. I'm grateful this table's marble. It makes me want to invest in one at home, but it's not very safe with small children running around. Maybe one in the office could be a very good idea.

"I love you, Petra."

"I love you, Mr. Shaw." I spank her ass. "Okay, I love you, Jack. I need a shower," she sighs.

"And some food."

"Yes, that sounds wonderful." I pull out of her and carry my lovely wife to the bathroom to clean up from the mess we made. I don't even give a fuck about the conference at all. It's the purpose of being here, but I can't seem to think past Petra's needs at the moment.

Given everything that happened last night and this morning, I doubt I'll be welcomed. People frown on caveman tendencies these days. Not that I give a fuck as long as my wife is happy, and she most certainly is. Everyone else can go fuck themselves.

Twelve

PETRA

I smile as we take the elevator into the office. We haven't encountered any other employees this morning, but I'm sure Jack is just waiting for his moment to brag. He'd probably take a conference call while drilling me on his desk.

"What has that smile on your face, Mrs. Shaw?"

I turn and look at my much taller husband and smirk. "I'm just thinking about your office desk right now."

With a groan, he adjusts his cock. "Wife, I'm supposed to get some work done."

"I promise I'll behave. Besides, we've been gone

too long, so there's much to do. Maybe after work you can give me a performance evaluation."

"Excellent suggestion." We exit the elevator and he walks me over to my desk.

Sliding his arm around my waist, he pulls me close and crushes his mouth to mine. We kiss until I hear something fall onto the floor.

"Oops. You better get to work, Mr. Shaw."

"I'm going to mark that ass of yours for that, my Pet."

"Promises. Now go." I rub the front of his crotch before spinning him toward his office.

"You'll pay for that."

"Add it to my eval." I wink and then sit behind my desk and turn on my computer. We have a dozen messages since I checked them last night. He told me to leave it, but I waited until today, I'd never get anything else done. Despite informing people that we'd be out of the office for the week, calls still came in.

I behave until lunch when I knock on my boss's office. He smiles and greets me while holding the door open. "What can I do for you?"

"I just wanted to let you know it's time for lunch and I was going to head down to the lunchroom." He drags me inside, slamming the door shut. My back hits the door, and his arms bracket my body. "Why would you need to do that, wife?"

"I'm hungry." I look at him with lustful eyes, knowing exactly what I'm doing.

"If you're hungry, I've got something to put in your mouth." He grabs me by my ponytail, drags me over to his desk, and then nudges me down to my knees while he takes a seat in his chair.

"Still hungry."

"Starving." I grab his belt and drag the leather through the loop. My pussy throbs in anticipation.

"Let me help you." He pulls out his thick length that's already completely hard and brushes it against my lips. "Open up wide." I take him down inch by inch until I'm gagging on his big, meaty cock.

"Fuck, my Pet, you're doing so well. Suck me like a good assistant and then I'll take you to lunch. You know I'm not going to let you have lunch with that prick."

I pop off his length, and moan, "My caveman."

"That's right. Now get under the desk. We have company."

"What?"

"You heard me." I slide under his desk, but I don't stop working his cock. There's a knock at the door.

"Come in," Jack barks, sounding irritated, but

now I know my husband's tone is full of lust.

"Sir, I brought up the mail, but Petra wasn't at the desk, so I thought I'd bring it in here." Elliot did show up here.

Jack grunts, "That's fine. Leave it on her desk. She'll be back in a moment. And Mr. Timmons, from now on refer to her as Mrs. Shaw."

"Mrs. Shaw?"

"Yes, she's mine." The authoritative sound in his voice sends desire through me and I suck harder on his cock. He groans and I'm not sure if Elliot notices but there's a distinct sense of tension in the room and in my husband.

"Yes, Sir."

Jack's office door closes and Jack slides his chair back pulling me up from under his desk.

"Bad girl." Quickly, I'm bent over his desk, my skirt lifted, and my panties yanked down my legs. "You need a lesson."

His hand comes down on my ass, sending a shockwave of pain and pleasure through me. Jack does it to the other side before sliding the tip along my slit, testing my entrance. The bulbous head moves up and down until it's sopping wet with my juices and then Jack pushes his way inside me.

I lurch forward, gripping the front edge of the

wood for purchase. The force of his thrusts rock the surface, sending everything scattering. "Jack, I'm coming."

"Good. Good because I'm coming too, my beautiful wife." He brushes my ponytail and loose hair to the side and begins sucking on my neck, kissing and biting my pulse as his seed floods my womb.

His large frame leans over mine before wrapping his arms around my waist and dragging me back onto his lap while he sits in his chair.

"My dear assistant, are you ready for lunch?"

"Are we taking a long lunch today?"

"I'm afraid I have a call this afternoon, so how about we order in and you can run the calls by me."

"Okay. Let me get freshened up and you order some Chinese. I have a taste for it today."

"Sure thing, my pet." He kisses my lips and I stand with my thighs all sticky from his release. Sliding up my panties, I head over to the bathrooms on this floor, get freshened up and go to my desk to get all the information I need.

Elliot brought up an entire bin of mail for me to go through, so I decide to take that with me. I can sort it in there while we go over his calls. I'm just about to carry it, when Jack takes it from me.

"Don't carry that. It's heavy as hell." His mouth is on mine and then the elevator door opens again. This time it's Linda from HR.

"Well, I brought up the documents you asked for, Mr. Shaw."

"Leave the mail here, Petra. We have some forms to fill out on top of the calls."

"Forms?"

"Yes, you're now part owner of Shaw Enterprises."

"I can't be."

"You're my wife, sweetheart."

"Still. I shouldn't be—"

He cuts me off. "The hell you shouldn't be my wife."

"I meant I shouldn't be owner. I don't deserve it."

"Well, you are anyway, but you can still be my assistant." He turns to Linda who is looking bemused. "I'll get these to you. Petra and I have a lot to do and time is slipping away from us today."

"Yes, Sir."

She leaves us and we head into the office. Five hours later we manage to get all the work done and then my husband gladly has to time to go over my performance evaluation, most thoroughly.

Epilogue

JACK

Did I just hear my wife correctly? She said another man was fine. I'm about to take her over my knee and spank her ass and then fuck her senseless. I might just have to fuck her in front of everyone to prove a damn point.

I wipe my hands off on the kitchen towel and walk into the living room where Val and Petra are talking about the baby's room. My wife is finally pregnant with our baby. For as much fucking as we were doing, I didn't knock her up right away. I've been waiting for a BJ for a bit, almost an entire year. Our one-year anniversary is coming up soon, but I won't be waiting another year. I have a baby Jack or Jill coming in seven months.

Granted, that's probably not going to be the name we pick, but my wife gets a kick out of saying she's going to give me a BJ. And I'll be grateful for whichever one it is, whether it's one where she's actually on her knees sucking my cock like a hungry queen, or an actual baby.

"Whose boss is fine?" I growl.

"Mine, darling."

"Good to hear," I remark, knowing she's full of shit. I didn't miss their conversation. I know it's all about Val's boss.

She just rolls her eyes at me, asking for a good spanking and fucking. I've been taking it easy on her since I found out we're having a baby, but now she's testing me. My dick is stiffening just considering the punishment of having her deep-throating me until she's gagging before I have her on all fours with my handprints on her bottom.

"Anyway, Valentine. Are you ever going to make a move on that man?" she asks her, sounding annoyed.

"Nope. He's my boss and completely out of my league. Besides, he's kind of the grumpiest man in existence. I don't know if you've heard. He's kind of a big deal and always on the news as the pain-in-the-ass lawyer with a winning record, gorgeous face even though he looks like he eats people for lunch." Given how instrumental her nosiness was in getting Petra to tempt me, she's being a bit hypocritical.

"Maybe you can get him to eat you for lunch." She wags her brows, shaking her bottom on Val's carpet. I want to laugh because apparently being pregnant makes her extremely horny. Not like she wasn't already insanely wild before, but the thought of her talking about another man gets me a bit jealous.

"Woman, leave the girl alone. Valentine, it's all fixed." I give my attention directly to my beautiful wife and grunt, "It's time to go and leave your friend alone. I have some plans for you, and a spanking to give you for even mentioning that Wyatt King is fine."

"What are you talking about?" she says, throwing her hands up, trying to lie while her face gives her away. She's grinning from ear to ear about her punishment. I'm going to enjoy it just as much.

"Don't lie, woman. You're terrible at it, and I'm only going to make your ass redder. So let's get going before I fuck you on the hood of the car so everyone knows you're taken." The thought has some merit if I weren't such a possessive husband.

I help her off the floor and wave to Val as I scoop her up in my arms, cradling her close to my chest. "Maybe you should stay away from King. Men like him are pure animals. They have this brooding exterior and poof, they let it out and bam, you're naked, married, pregnant, and orgasming every damn hour," she huffs out, but I know her ass is grinning from ear to ear without having to tilt my head down to look. I swat her ass just as we walk out the door because I'm on a mission to prove a point to my wife.

I can hear Val call out, "Have fun."

Oh, we will.

I help her into the SUV and then buckle her in just so I could steal a kiss from her pouty lips before I run around and get into my seat.

With a grunt, I say, "I need you naked and ready the second we get through the door. You're going to be in for it."

"Promises, promises." She scoffs like she doesn't believe me.

Shaking my head, I chuckle and then pull out on the road. "Keep that shit up and see if I don't make you cry from too many orgasms." It's only happened once, and I was actually surprised by her reaction and so was she. Then again, it was her eighth in a row.

That's her limit. When it comes to pleasing her, I have no limit. I live for Petra Shaw.

Everything I do now is for her, even driving to Val's shitty apartment—or rather their old apartment—to fix a leaky faucet because Val doesn't want to take a handout and get a better place, and the girls wanted to hang out.

It actually works well for the both of us. She gets the quality time she needs with her best friend, and I get to make sure she's safe while working with my hands. It's been a long time since I've had a chance to do things like that.

Since Petra came into my life, I've started delegating tasks so I have more time for her, and now I'm going to be working on hiring another executive so I'll be able to take more time off for my family that's growing as we speak. A sense of pride fills me knowing that our baby is growing inside of her.

"Hey, you keep that magic tongue at bay and we won't have to have that problem."

"Well, then, you behave."

She tilts her head and her lips twist upward into an adorable pout. "You know that's hard for me."

"Well, it's hard for me when you taste so fucking good and I love eating your pretty cunt until you give me all that damn juice and your voice sings my name."

We pull into the driveway of our home outside of the city about twenty minutes from Val's so the girls can stay close and I have quick access to the expressways to get to the office. We bought a new house two months ago, and it's massive so we can grow our large family.

"It's time to pay for your mouth and with your mouth, my wife," I say. She giggles and makes a dash out of the vehicle.

"You have to catch me first, Mr. Shaw," she shouts, running with her coat open. I'm going to spank her for sure. It's the middle of February and chilly outside. Luckily the snow has melted, but I'll forever be protective of my wife.

"Whoa. Hold up, I don't want you to fall."

"I'm fine." She rolls her eyes and hurries up our porch. Once she's through the door, I'm steps behind her. I watch her as she removes her coat and shoes, but she's still moving up the stairs. I follow suit, stripping as I make my way to my wife.

By the time I get to my bedroom, Petra's on the floor just inside our room on her knees with her hair in a ponytail, completely naked but for the rings I slid on her finger. I stand there in just my boxer briefs, dick impression clearly trying to tear through the cotton.

"Someone's a horny little thing," I growl, attempting to catch my breath and take in the sight before me. My tongue swipes over my bottom lip as I stare in fascination.

"I am."

"It's not much of a punishment if you want it," I remind her.

"Fine, I'll just take care of myself." She reaches down and starts teasing one hand on her breast while the other dips into her pussy.

I shake my head as I charge forward. "No. Stop. Those hands belong on me. I want them wrapped around my cock and balls. Now." Petra freezes for a moment, pulling her fingers from her wet hole.

With gusto, she takes my shaft in her hands and strokes it once before sliding her mouth over it as her sticky fingers gently massage my balls. She pulls on them just enough to cause a little pain before letting go and then she pulls off my cock to lick my nuts.

A subtle smile appears on her face because I'm so ready to blow, and she knows it. I'm the one supposed to be torturing her, and she's the one trying to unman me.

I grip her hair in my hand and demand to let go.

"Be a good girl and get on the bed. I want to fuck that pretty cunt." She smiles up at me with her lips pursed. Before she stands, she kisses the tip. With a sway of her hips, she moves into position onto the bed on all fours.

I climb up behind her and test her entrance. Her hole is nice and slippery, but I'm not ready to pounce just yet. I want her primed and ready to cream all over my cock the second I get inside because my dick is going to explode the moment it's wrapped up in her silky sheath.

Bending down, I lick her seam, tasting her soaking wet hole all the way up to her pucker. I bite her cheek before giving her another smack on her pretty ass, loving the way she moans for more. I thrust into her sweet heat and fuck her womb until she comes for me.

I work her warmth all night, driving into her over and over to remind her who she belongs to and that she's Mrs. Jack Shaw.

Epilogue

PETRA

FIVE YEARS LATER

Three boys. We have three boys all running amok in the house while I try to handle the paperwork. I'm still Jack's assistant, but now he only works four days a week and I only work six-hour days instead of a full ten like he does, so I get more time to take care of the boys. We have a daycare facility in the building and our boys are there a couple times a week, but our oldest, Carter, is about to start kindergarten.

Next month Jack's new assistant will take my place. He's a nice guy, although Jack doesn't like that

I have to do a lot of the training, but like I remind him, the man would be more attracted to my husband than me.

"My pet, where are you?" His voice still does the same thing to me as if I'm hearing it for the first time. I want to be in his arms, aching to be kissed, but I try to remain cool and relaxed.

"In our office," I call out, setting my bare feet up on the desk. I hear his steady footsteps before he reaches the door. "Hello, handsome." My expression doesn't give away that I'm practically panting with lust, but if he checked, he'd know.

"God, you look gorgeous." He tilts his head and stares at me from the doorway with his arms crossed and sleeves rolled up, revealing the taut muscles on his strong forearms. You'd never know that this man sat behind a desk. My eyes linger on his buff arms and chest a little longer than they should, but I can't fight the pull.

"Why, thank you, Mr. Shaw. It's been wonderful working for you. It's a shame that my time has come to an end," I say with a playful pout because I'm sure I'll find a reason to sneak into his office.

"It truly has. I've never had such an incredibly talented assistant." He moves in closer, and I know I'm going to be thoroughly fucked because his eyes are laser-focused on me with the same pure lust I'm giving him.

I smile and shake my head. "Yes, Mr. Shaw, but you see, I have a lot of work to handle before I call it quits. I'd hate for my boss to be upset with me."

"I promise you he will not be upset if you give me your time and your body. He'll be extremely appreciative…extremely appreciative." I squeal when he pounces, pulling me out of my chair with lightning speed. His mouth crushes mine. "He'll most certainly approve."

Jack lifts me onto his desk, sending my pencil skirt rising up my thighs, revealing the edge of my ass. "I'm going to ruin his notes."

He looks down and sees my panties are wet. "Fuck, I'll just have to reprint them." He runs his thick finger over my fabric-covered slit and my entire body vibrates with need for more. His hand snakes over the edge of my panties and down until he's cupping my cunt while pushing two fingers inside. "Give me a kiss, Mrs. Shaw."

"Yes, Mr. Shaw," I stammer as my feet flex from the sensations.

"Such a good wife." With a flex of his fingers, I nearly come off the desk. "So fucking responsive." I need to come, but I want his big cock inside me, working me, stretching me, breaking me in two.

"Will you fuck me, Mr. Shaw?" I arch my back, rolling my hips to send his fingers deeper into me. God, it's so incredible. It's bliss when he touches me. From the first dominating day, Jack has owned me and I'll never get enough.

"Why, that sounds like a great idea, my pet."

He pulls his fingers out and brings them to his mouth, sucking my sticky mess off them which makes my pussy clench with desire and hunger. I gently push him back and drop to my knees. "Are you hungry for my dick, my pet?" he asks, freeing his cock from his dress pants.

"Yes, Mr. Shaw." I lick my lips and squeeze my breasts to help ease the ache, but it only makes me crave more. I grip his length and suck his huge rod down my throat, working his shaft as if I'll never get this thick, sexy, engorged dick again.

Like he knows just what I need, he wraps my ponytail around my hair. "Suck harder, wife."

I do as he says, taking him harder and deeper, running my tongue underneath along the large vein. "Fuck, Petra. You're such a dirty little assistant. I expect you to visit my office every damn day."

I pull off his cock to ask, "Then why do you need an assistant?"

"Because he's there for work, and you, my sexy wife, are there for pleasure."

"Maybe I'll consider it."

"I'll persuade you," he offers. "Now, either continue taking me down your throat, or you can bend over the desk and take me deep." I suck on his huge length once more, but my husband has had enough. With a rough grunt, he grips my arms and lifts me off my feet and spins me around, setting me on my stomach on the desk. He slams into me in one smooth motion.

"Mr. Shaw," I moan, turning my head to give him a smile.

"Fuck, you're so damn beautiful." He leans down and kisses my throat. "I love you, Petra."

"I love you, Jack," I cry out, squeezing my pussy around him, coaxing our orgasms. We rock the heavy wood desk as he fucks me hard and rough with his hands moving over my hips and up to my breasts. He gives them a squeeze before he rips my blouse, freeing my tits from the bra with a quick tug downward on the lace material.

I nearly come as the cool air hits my chest. Then

Jack pinches my nipple and I'm done, flexing and creaming all over his cock.

"That's it, Petra. I love the way you come all over me. Now take it; take my load." He bites my shoulder until he roars, sending jets of cum into my pussy. He pulls us back onto the chair, leaving himself inside me as I sit on his lap. I twist my upper body slightly and kiss his lips. Once I break our kiss, I press my sweat-covered forehead on his shoulder and rest while he rubs my back.

"You're everything to me, Petra. I'm going to miss seeing you for hours at a time."

"I'll stop by whenever you want."

"Thank you, my love." We kiss and begin round two.

An hour later, my dirty boss is quite pleased with his assistant and very grateful.

"Where are the boys?" I ask as we get dressed and leave our office.

"I asked my sister to watch them. You and I have a few hours to ourselves, but she's still mad at me for not inviting her to our wedding," he mutters that last bit out, knowing it's a bit ridiculous.

"That was five years ago," I remind him.

"Yeah, well, she can hold a grudge, so she's going

to send them back full of sugar." I roll my eyes because it's nothing she hasn't done before.

"What's new?" I roll my eyes because his sister is hilariously sweet. She's a baker, and of course she fills them with sugar. It's never too much, but still, they're little and it doesn't take much for them to be riled up. Either way, we don't care because Daddy loves to wear them out before we put them to bed.

"Nothing, but she wanted us to know."

"That's fine as long as I'm filled with cream," I say, grabbing for his belt again.

"I've always got plenty for you, my pet, my love, my wife."

A Best Friends Duet:

Picture Perfect * Instant Obsession

Best Friends Series:

Always You * His Dirty Secret * Sleep Tight

Bianchi Crime Family:

Married to the Mob * Captured by the Mob * Owned by the Mob

Cavanaugh Security Series:

Protecting Macy * Securing Blake

The Cline Brothers of Colorado:

Whatever it Takes * Finding Paradise

Dirty Boss Series:

My Pet * My Cookie * My Flower

The Falling Series:

Falling for the Boss * Falling for the Enemy * Falling Hard

The Fiore Family:

Christmas with the Beast * Christmas with the Boss

Christmas with the Sheriff

Gimme Series:

Sugar * Luck * Rain * Cream * Heat * Love

The James Family:

No Choice * No Way Out * No More Waiting

Keepsakes:

Keeping Blossom * Keep in Mind

The Lamian Wars:

Bound * Reveal * Release

All Hallows Eve

The Middleton Hotels:

Built for Me * Built to Last * Built Strong

Built Over Time * Built Overnight

Nothing but Trouble Series:

Taking the Bait * Taking the Mafia Princess

The O'Connell Family:

Claiming Red * Burning for Claire

Claiming Abby * Reminding Red

Obsessed Alpha Series:

Stone * Cole * Graham

Theo * Maddox *Alessandro

Tony * Cormack * Cameron

Reynolds Ranch Series:

Lara * Tobias

A Rocky Start Series:

Rocky Waters * Her Rock * Rocky Start

A Rough Hands Novella:

My Miracle * Nailing my Wife

Say Something Series:

Say Uncle *Say Please * Say Uncle: Doggy Style

Second Generation:

Say Yes

Sister Switch:

Testing Her Professor * Assisting Her Boss

A Steele Christmas:

Mason's Winter * Perfectly Wrapped * The Company You Keep

A Steele Fairy Tale:

My Gold * My Forever

My Property * My Prince Charming

A Steele Riders Family Novella Series:

Holiday Knockout * His Siren

Steele Riders MC Series:

Boomer * Mick * Jackson * Doc * Beast * Ghost

Wrench * Blade * Boss * Cowboy * Law

Southern Hospitality:

Down South * Gone South

Sweetheart's Treats:

Sweet Surprise * Doctor's Orders, Sweetheart * Sweet Surrender

Twin Sin:

Stalk Me Please * Sinful Intent

White Wolf Ridge Series:

Turner

Wolfe Creek Series:

Wolfe's Den * Beta: Her Alpha

Raging Kane * Written in History

Standalones:

Buying Love * Conquering Alexandria * Ecstasy Captured

Grant's Deal * In Heat * Intense * Killer Abs * Love Discovered

Loving My Neighbor * Mrs. Valentine * My Christmas Gift

Rainy Days * Stormy Nights * Red Hot Nights

Room Service * Scarred * Sharp Curves

So Wrong * Standing There * The Mobster's Virgin

The Wedding Guest * Unexpected